MW00389507

Copyright © 2018 Saquion Gullett

Contact@GullettWrites.com

- This is a work of fiction. Names, characters, businesses, places, events, locales, and incidents are either the products of the author's imagination or used in a fictitious manner. Any resemblance to actual persons, living or dead, or actual events is purely coincidental.

*** - Denotes a change of tense.

Chapter 1

MEMORY LANE

Everything that Lock has worked for since he was 5 years old has led him here. He woke up way earlier than he ever wanted to for 13 years and then stressed himself one step away from a mental asylum for the next four. That's all over now and he can not wrap his head around finally graduating from college. He does, though, think about it constantly. The idea of it doesn't seem strange, but he knows that life is going to be so much different without books, tests and essays to write. He's excited that his

GrandPop is making the trip down. Old age and declining health have caused the once adventurous man to rarely leave New Jersey these days. Lock's best friend Castle is flying down also, making it even more of a cause for celebration.

As happy and excited as Lock is today, there's a tinge of sadness that he carries with him. The kind of sadness that never truly leaves a person, and sometimes shows up for a split second even in moments of blissful joy. The sadness is that his Mother won't see him get his degree. She passed away last year from a lung condition. She got caught up in the streets pretty early, and it took a toll on her body. Not long after she stopped smoking crack and drinking alcohol for good, she found out that she was sick. Lock's mother kept her serious illness a secret from him. Now Lock is normally as sharp as a whip, but that quality hides from him in end of life scenarios and he didn't pick up on the signs. It haunts him constantly as he feels that he should have been able to see it. He went to see her in the hospital the day before she died. He thought that she would be fine and flew back to school. "How could I be so stupid? So naive?" he thinks. He feels that he will never totally get past it. The onslaught of grief is quickly pushed away by a sudden beam of pride. He feels as if he knows that she is proud of him today and in the microsecond that it took that thought to creep in, it changes Lock's whole mood. Maybe he'll get a sign that she is with him at his graduation tonight.

Tomorrow will introduce Lock to a new challenge with a familiar face. He is heading back to Jersey for a while. It's kind of stupid to leave Atlanta where everything in rap music is happening to go back to the town where he grew up. His Grand Pop is sick though and he needs Lock around. Still reeling from the loss of his Mom, he doesn't know how long his Grand Pop will live and he is vowing to not make the same mistake twice. Lock kind of misses Salem anyway. He doesn't know why because there is nothing there-not many jobs, most of the stores are closed, and a lot of the houses are abandoned. Even with all of that, he has so much pride in being from there. Everyone that grew up there hates so much about it, but love it too, with every fiber in their bodies. It's weird but true. Lock figures that while he is there he will do most of his music dealings in Philly since it's the closest big city. Plus, Philly is poppin' right now!

Salem, NJ is a small town in the state's southwestern area. A once industrial haven as far as small towns go, with multiple factories that employed the residents and a bustling downtown section with shops and restaurants at every turn. By the mid

-1990's when Lachlan Wilds was born, Salem had seen better days. Then a burgeoning ghetto, the factories had mostly closed and the future looked bleak. Everyone held tight to the memories of Salem's glory days seemingly ignoring the road ahead.

Present day, Salem's story reads like that of most inner cities in America. White flight was followed by a drying up of resources, at the same time drug use spread like wildfire and crime skyrocketed. Lachlan, or "Lock" as he is called, managed to sidestep the many pitfalls that were waiting for him. He not only finished high school but also went away to college and became the first person in his family to earn a degree. He is on his way back to Salem to care for his ailing Grandfather while also looking to build the small fledgling record label that he started before college into a serious hit maker.

Lock sets foot in Salem and he feels like the president. He stops by all of the hangout spots and everybody is showing him love. Handshakes and hugs are almost always followed by offers of free alcohol and the chance to hit the blunt. He thinks to himself that this must be what it's like when someone first gets home from jail. People coming home from school don't usually get the same outpouring of love and applause. Crazy but true.

A couple of months pass and by now Lock begins to feel settled in. The newness of being back home has worn off, and it is a lot easier to focus on his business. Things have been pretty calm on the surface, but like the locally infamous riptides and undercurrents on the bank of the Delaware River which borders Salem on the west side, what's brewing underneath is powerful and violent. Invisible to the eye, but almost certain death once met.

Lock wakes early just about every day. He is up extra early today but lays in bed contemplating his future. Not only does he have an important meeting today, but he also feels like he is at a pivotal point in his business. These next few months could make or break him. He is hopeful but apprehensive, a born eternal optimist mixed with the pessimism that slowly creeps into the consciousness of every child of any ghetto. After laying there for well over an hour, he finally rises to get his day started.

First he showers, always with music blaring, and water near scorching. In fact, the water is so hot that when he opens the door to leave the bathroom it frequently triggers the smoke alarms. He gets dressed while either watching TV or listening to music. Today he's listening to music. He feels that music can help put him in the necessary mood and mental state for any particular day, so he picks songs accordingly. Today, feeling like the savvy young businessman, Jay Z gets the nod. After getting dressed he grabs his phone to check his emails and browse social media. Normally he grabs his phone as soon as he opens his eyes, but today is a bit different.

Lock heads to the living room to sit down and read one of his books. Sometimes he reads multiple books at once, but he doesn't read quickly by any account, so one chapter per day is plenty. He still has a few hours until his meeting so now seems like the perfect chance.

After being buried in the book for quite some time, the silence is broken by the sound of the knob of his front door turning. Lock stands up and heads toward the door, in no rush to get there before it opens. The door cracks somewhat slowly, but then swings open rather abruptly, almost jerky. Stumbling through the entrance is Donovan Castle, everyone calls him "Castle" for short. He and Lock have been best friends since the 1st grade when they met in Mrs. Powers' class. They fought during recess that first week of school, and have been inseparable ever since.

Once Lock notices Castle as his welcomed intruder, he turns mid-step and heads back to the couch where he had been sitting. Both Castle and Lock stopped knocking before entering each other's houses years ago.

"What's goin' on?" Lock asks.

"I'm good bro. How about you?"

Lock replies that he is doing fine also, and no sooner than the words roll off of his tongue, Castle screams

"Oh shit!" while looking down at his phone. Half-startled, Lock asks Castle about what he sees. He replies,

"A couple people got hit on Sinnick."

Which is short for Sinnickson Street, one of Salem's longstanding drug blocks. Castle continues to say,

"They said it's mad cops out there and they got the block taped off."

Lock picks up his phone to see what he can find out also, while simultaneously asking,

"Did they say anything about who it is?"

Castle says he doesn't see anything extra details yet.

While both scouring the internet and sending out texts to get more information on the shooting, the conversation shifts to their plans for the day.

"Not too much right now, I got a meeting at noon though with Scott Campbell." Lock states.

Castle asks, "What is that about?"

Lock's face begins to light up with excitement, and with a bit of slyness he says, "Old money. He lights his stove with the type of bread that can take us to the next level. We need him backing us."

Castle, seeming a bit unimpressed responds, "Let's just get at a dollar and take ourselves to the next level. We could take this label money, grab a brick, flip it a couple times and be back like we never left!"

"Absolutely not!" Lock states intensely. "On top of the 100 reasons why that's a bad idea, you promised me you would be done with this street shit 6 months ago. If we are gonna be businessmen, we can't have that cloud over top of us. Shit like that always comes back to bite you at the worst possible time."

Castle, almost dismissive of the previous statement, rebuts with, "So are you saying gangsters can't be businessmen? Stop being scary bro. Behind every great fortune was a great crime. I trust your smarts bro, but you gotta trust me too sometimes."

Looking a tad bit dejected by Castle's comments, Lock looks at him and while gently but quickly tapping his own temple says, "You have to think bigger than these narrow streets bro. There is a whole world out there that is begging to be taken. Your vision is too limited and it's looking like it can be a liability."

Like he was made of Teflon, Castle lets Lock's words slide right off of him, then he says, "Don't forget that half of this company got started off of that same liability money. It was good enough then, but not now huh?"

Lock Sternly replies, "Definitely not now! Using it as part of start-up funding is one thing. Backtracking into it full throttle in the middle is completely different. Let's talk about this later though. I have to head to this meeting."

Lock arrives at his meeting 27 minutes early. Sometimes he shows up an hour early or even more. Lock isn't a street guy by far, but he idolizes the characters in gangster movies, and since Jimmy Conway from the movie "Goodfellas" showed up to his meeting with Henry Hill over an hour early, Lock does the same thing. In some small way, it makes him feel empowered. Like an omni-intelligent mob boss who always out thinks the person on the other side of the table. Lock sits there in a daze for several minutes and his eyes glaze over as he daydreams about gangland shootouts and witty one-liners. Finally, he is jolted out of his open-eyed slumber by a cool but powerful voice saying to him,

"Lachlan, I'm glad that we could meet today."

As Lock snaps out of it, he looks up to see a hand extended toward him already awaiting the ceremonial shake. Lock quickly stands and extends his hand as well. He is careful to squeeze tightly, but not too tight-he wants to exude strength, but it is important that it also seems effortless. He looks the man directly in his clear blue eyes and for a nanosecond marvels at the unique hue. They must be contacts he thinks to himself because Cal Ripken's eyes aren't even that light.

The man standing before Lock is Scott Campbell. At slightly over 6 foot 2 inches, he's not extremely towering, but the confidence that flows from him gives onlookers the illusion of an 8-foot giant. His shoulders are broad and his skin is by design slightly tanned, accented superbly by his blue suit and power tie which looks nice but is far from what he, as a multi-millionaire, can actually afford. There's not a curl to be found in his slicked-back strawberry blonde hair, and his 5 O'clock shadow looks like it took a lifetime to perfect.

"Have a seat." Lock states as he motions toward the empty chair across the table from where he is now beginning to sit down.

As both men are seated, Lock notices that Scott is wearing a Movado watch. Again, nice but far under what his bank account affords. He doesn't spend money just because he can.

"So, Mr. Campbell"

Scott interrupts Lock in mid-sentence "Call me Scott, Mr. Campbell is my father."

"OK, Scott, let me start by saying that I'm really happy that you could meet with me today. I am excited about what the future holds for Sale City Music, and I believe that our interests can be mutually beneficial."

Scott replies "I believe so as well, I do have a few questions if you don't mind."

Lock nods in agreement while trying to hold back his eagerness to delve deeper into the conversation.

"How do you believe that I can help you, and in turn what would be the benefits for me if this relationship were to take off?" Scott asks.

"Well as I am sure that you know, I have been able to take this very small imprint, which began as nothing more than an idea, and turn it into a respected brand. We have put together successful events all over the Tri-State area."

Seemingly unmoved by Lock's statement Scott quickly asks,

"What plans do you have for expansion? I mean, the Tri-State area is nice, but I'm sure you have bigger sights than that."

Lock produces a few pieces of paper from a folder sitting on the table. As he hands them to Scott he begins to say,

" Based on these projections with the numbers that we have already produced, if we add that to the solid ROI scale and end it with the well-oiled exit strategy, I'd say you can't lose on this Scott."

Somewhat cryptically, Scott responds,

"Loss is at the table on every deal. Wise men create plans that cut him out of the share."

"Which is why preparation has made this a sure thing. Well, as close to a sure thing as possible." Lock replies.

"Loss is also a glutton who feeds on the arrogant. I like what you're doing, but I need some time to think it over. I must say, through all of your planning, your lack of a flagship artist is really troubling to me. Bring me a star in the making and I can almost promise that you have a deal." Scott states while getting up from the table and buttoning the top button of his suit jacket.

"I look forward to speaking with you when you are more prepared. Have a good day Lachlan."

Scott reaches out for a handshake and Lock obliges.

Lock smiles and nods as he and Scott promise to speak soon as they begin to part ways. On the outside Lock looks happy and confident, but on the inside, he is slowly dying as he questions his performance in the meeting. As he turns to walk to his car he thinks to himself,

"Damn it! How could I be so stupid?! I hope I didn't blow it. I should have opened up differently, I should have focused more on what we have accomplished. What was I thinking to bring that stupid ass Tri-State shit?"

Lock opens his car door and drops into the seat like a sack of potatoes, he loosens his tie and unbuttons the top button of his shirt. He pounds the steering wheel with his fist three times in rapid succession. He then looks into the rearview mirror and directly into his own eyes and tells himself to suck it up.

Aside from feeling like he completely botched the meeting with Scott Campbell, there is something else bothering Lock. An intuition is brewing in the back of his mind, but he hasn't given himself any time to think about it. He hasn't even clarified in his own mind what this feeling in his gut is tied to. Lock drives around for the next 10 minutes with no direction. He debates on going to get food but decides to put that off until after he stops by to visit Reena.

Chapter 2

FAMILY FEUD

On the corner of Broadway and Market Street in Salem, there lies a metal star made of brass embedded into the concrete. To all Salem residents, it is aptly known as Star Corner. Legend has it that in 1820 Robert Gibbon Johnson ate a basket full of tomatoes there to disprove a common fear of the day that tomatoes were poisonous. In actuality the story is true, but the location was just across the street on the steps of the county courthouse. Either way, Star Corner is also the place where Lock and his cosmic twin Reena Elanor had the fight that nearly ended their all but unbreakable lifelong friendship way back when they were both in the 7th grade.

It was a hot sunny Saturday the first week of June. It hadn't rained in over 3 weeks. The cement sidewalks and asphalt streets trapped the heat like a brick oven. Reena asked Lock to walk with her to the post office where she was meeting her friend Milan who had a copy of the application she needed to attend a summer program at the community college. After complaining for 15 minutes about walking in the heat, Lock gave in and the two headed up 7th Street and onto Broadway toward the post office. As they approach the corner where Broadway meets Market Street, they are stopped by a flow of cars who have the green light to pass by. Lock gazes across to Star Corner and decides to have some fun at Reena's expense.

There is another legend of Star Corner that the citizens of Salem speak of. A tall tale shrouded in superstition. The lore is that anyone who steps on the star is bound to live in the confines of the city for the rest of their days. As Reena's closest confidant, Lock knows that Reena is terribly superstitious and deathly afraid of stepping on the star. Lock thinks it would be a nice laugh to push her onto the star, forcing her to get over such a stupid phobia.

As they walk across the intersection and approach the star, Lock slows down just a bit so that he is ever so slightly behind while flanking Reena to her right side. He knows that once she gets close to the star that she will detour with extreme caution. Just as she begins to side-step the star Lock hip checks her while she still has one foot off of the ground. As soon as their midsections collide, he also pushes off with both hands sending Reena flying directly towards the star. What Lock couldn't have known is just how deep Reena's fear goes. Instead of planting her foot on the star to break her fall, Reena chose instead to tumble over the star landing with a loud thud to the scorching hot red brick sidewalk of West Broadway. Without the foot to balance her body, Reena's shoulder took the brunt of the fall and the skin scraped off so deep that it didn't bleed for 2 minutes. Her knee didn't fare much better than her shoulder and her opposite wrist was sprained. After that, she didn't speak to Lock until the middle of August even though he tried to apologize at least twice a week all summer long.

Those scars have since healed and the events of that day hold no bearings on their bond today, other than the fact that Reena brings it up every chance she gets as a sympathy card and a bargaining tool whenever she needs to. A well which seems to never run dry.

***

A ritual takes place whenever Lock approaches Reena's door. He knocks in the same cadence every time, four taps in two quick sets of two. Tap tap..tap tap. He then immediately turns the knob. If the door is unlocked he walks right in. Reena is wiping the top of her glass living room table in a circular motion with crumpled up newspaper-a technique that her Grandmother taught her when she was ten years old. Damp cloths leave smudges and lint, but newspaper leaves the glass looking flawless. She looks up from her masterful work as Lock enters the room.

"Hey!"

"Sup Ree? What are you doing?"

She replies, "Nothing much, just cleaning up. You know I'm OCD'ish."

"Yeah yeah, I know. Do you wanna go to Pat's with me?" Lock replies.

"I would, but Milan called and she's about to come by."

Lock falls on to the couch and puts his hands up to his head looking somewhat dejected.

Reena asks, "Everything OK?"

"I don't know what it is, but my Spidey senses are tingling. I've had this sinking feeling in my gut all week that I just can't put my finger on. I feel like Castle is somehow gonna sink my ship because he just don't get it. Not that he can't, or that he ain't smart enough. He don't wanna get it."

Reena stops what she's doing to focus on the conversation. "Why don't you just cash him out and do the label on your own.

The last word is barely off of her tongue before Lock says "I can't do that."

"Why not? I'm not saying to stop being his friend."

Lock sits up and becomes more engaged in the conversation.

"So I should take away his one chance at making it out of here? We both know that without this, all he got is those streets that he loves so much. The streets are undefeated. How can I stand back and let my best friend get lost in a fight that I know he can't win?"

Reena rebuts with, "I understand that you are super loyal. It is one of the things that I've always loved about you. You can't let it be your downfall though. Now maybe we're getting too deep because this is just a feeling that you're having, but the best thing that you can do for Castle is to keep yourself in a position to save him from himself."

"I see what you are saying." Lock replies.

Reena lightens up the mood by saying,

"Plus, if you don't make all of those millions then who's going to buy me that Ferrari that I just have to have?"

"Oh it's a Ferrari now? Changes every month huh? Maybe I might. I could just grab you like the illest Saturn ever!"

Lock rises up, and Reena stands as well. She playfully hits him on his shoulder and back. "Boy, don't play with me."

Forcing words through his full-on laugh Lock says "I have to go, I'll call you later. I have a lot of running around to do."

Almost immediately there is a light thumping at the door. Lock answers the door as he leaves. Whisking through the doorway is Reena's best friend Milan White.

It is painfully obvious that she's flirting when she says,

"Hi Lock!"

"Hey Milan. Are you coming to my party next week?"

She does a quick hoochie dance and says,

"I sure am. I get the VIP treatment right?"

As Lock feverishly types on his iPhone, he says,

"No doubt, just let me know how many you have with you."

Again, in a not so subtle attempt at flirtation, Milan replies with a somewhat drawn out "Ummm, hmmm."

Lock, so preoccupied with his phone, doesn't seem to catch on to the advance and in a very bland voice says,

"OK, I'll see y'all later."

Reena and Milan head to the kitchen for a glass of wine while they converse the routine topics of any given day-politics, Love & Hip Hop and the latest episode of who's fucking who in Salem.

In a break from the norm, Milan starts the conversation off by continuing to pine over Lock.

"Lock sure was looking good. You should give him my number girl.

"I don't think that's a good idea." Reena replies along with a slight eye-roll

Milan's brows bend just a bit and she looks up and down as she stated,

"And why not?"

"Because Milan."

"Because what, Reena? Just cause you two have this fake magical love affair ever since you were kids that you say you never acted on. You claim to be just friends, so if you really don't want him, then why can't anyone else have him?"

Reena takes in a deep breath.

"I just don't want it to cause any problems. You're my friend, he is my friend, and it can turn into a

whole disaster."

"Well if you are just friends like you say, then you won't mind your friends being friends. It's not my fault if he lose his mind after he get his hands on this!"

Reena is clearly not going along but laughs it off as she says,

"Oh god! I can't with you. Just leave Lock alone."

"OK, but only because you're my girl, and you clearly want to give it to him no matter what you say."

To say that the relationship between Reena and Lock is complicated would be an understatement on par with referring to the Rock of Gibraltar as a stone or The

Matterhorn a hill. Lock grew up on 7th Street, and Reena a few houses down and around the corner on Grant. When they were 4 years old Reena's family moved to Salem from Oregon. They instantly became friends and rode big wheels together. The next year when they were kindergarteners at John Fenwick School, Lock decided to impress Reena by asking his grandfather to take the training wheels off of his bike. It ended terribly. He fell six times before managing to stay upright for a smooth ride which lasted a few short seconds before plowing face first into the neighbor's SUV. Six stitches later, Reena was right there waiting for him when he got back from the hospital.

The next year in 1st grade, the universe would usher in a new dynamic to their blossoming affinity. It would come in the form of a push, a few crocodile tears and a fist fight. Six-year-old boys seldom find the words to tell a girl that they like them. So during recess on just the third day of school, a boy by the name of Donovan Castle pushed Reena clean off of the monkey bars. In his mind, on only its sixth trip around the sun, Donovan thought that they would go on to marry and live happily ever after. Instead, Reena crashed to the ground in a heap and screamed like Marion Crane in the shower. No knives were present, but by the ear-piercing shrill cry, one would be easily mistaken. Lock, not far away on the sliding board, receives Reena's scream like a blaring trumpet summoning a soldier to the battlefield. He storms in the direction of the monkey bars with as much reckless abandon as his 6-year-old frame could muster. He reached up, grabbed Donovan by his legs and ripped him from his perch, pulling so hard that Donovan knocks Lock down on his way to the ground. It takes a second for Donovan to realize that he is under siege, but it became apparently clear by the headlock and repetitious strikes to the face that he absorbs. He manages to free his head and get in a shot or two of his own before the teachers intervene. When the smoke settles both Lock and Donovan are suspended for 3 days. Upon returning to school Mrs. Powers gave them a group assignment forcing them to work together. They have been the next best thing to Siamese twins ever since.

As the trio reach adolescence the normal order of things is that Castle constantly and faithfully pursues Reena, who is far too transfixed on her friendship with Lock to ever give the flame that Castle carries for her any of the oxygen that it needs to flourish. Like everyone else, Castle feels the permeating energy of the bewitching power that Lock has over Reena and vice versa. That force can only be equally matched by an enigma best described as a Rubix cube of undefined emotions. Destined to remain platonic or turn physical is a burning question that neither knows the answer to nor do they care to address it with each other or themselves.

Such an intricate working is these three lives. Of course, they have carried on romantic relationships outside of their friendship, but their partners always end up jealous and the courtships never last. Reena's boyfriends always accuse her of Lock, and in return, he has never had a girlfriend that truly accepts her. Castle, true to form, can never totally veneer his lifelong pining for Reena while in the presence of his flavor of the moment.

Reena has the uncanny ability to parry Castle's advances without it becoming awkward and that allows them to remain friends. The real glue that keeps them together is their mutual love for Lock. Their equal allegiance to him keeps them in many ways close to each other even when he's not around.

Last year when Lock was away at school, Castle met and exchanged numbers with a woman from Penns Grove at a bar. After about a week and a half of texting the two decided to go to a movie. The original plan was for Saturday, but at the last minute, his date, Jasmine, had to reschedule. They settled on Monday night and everything went according to plan. Castle chose Deptford AMC because it's usually pretty quiet during the week and he figured that no one would be in his business. They arrive early enough that even after getting popcorn and candy they were first in the theater. This was by design as Castle always prefers to sit in the middle seat of the dead last row, and the earlier he gets there the better his chances of doing so.

The previews finally begin and Castle unburies his head from his phone. He chats with Jasmine a little about the events of their respective weekends as people slowly file into the theater. A few minutes pass and Castle, who would be considered by most a hypebeast, has his attention completely snatched by a Louis Vuitton supreme hoodie. He is so enamored by the shirt that it takes him a few seconds to realize who was wearing it-Priest, who grew up in Salem also. Priest was a monster on the basketball court and had a bunch of D1 offers, but got caught with drugs and a gun just before Thanksgiving of his senior year. He and Castle aren't friends, but they know each other pretty well, and as Priest makes his way up the theater stairs he notices Castle in the last row. For a split second, they make eye contact like two cowboys in the center of town at high noon. No words were exchanged, but a conversation took place between the two young men. An exchange that put Castle dead in the middle of a rock and a hard place. Priest dated Reena in high school. They'd broken up but had been back together for about a year. Despite loving Reena since elementary school, Castle never disliked Priest; however, watching him walk in with a statuesque female with feed-in braids and impeccably laid baby hairs, and who looked like she has at least 100 thousand Instagram followers won't get Priest into Castle's good graces.

For most people thrust into the position Castle was now in, the internal struggle would be to either keep quiet or spill the beans. For Castle, it was never a question. He would never tell. He loves Reena a lot, and this could have easily ended her relationship. With Lock away at school, it would have been his shoulder that she cried on. Even while knowing that, Castle could never bring himself to do such a thing. In his mind, guys who run and tell what they saw are corny and weak, so his internal struggle was wondering if he could still consider himself a good friend while knowing he would never let what he witnessed pass through his lips.

Reena would eventually find out even in Castle's silence. One of the hairdressers at the salon where Reena gets her hair done happened to be exiting a showing when she saw Priest enter with the other woman. When Reena came in for her next appointment, she told her every detail, right down to what color the girl's fingernails were painted. When Reena confronted Priest, he denied ever being at the theater but she persisted. The more he deflected, the more frustrated Reena became until eventually, she threw her soda at the side of his head. Orange liquid splashed all over the inside of his pristinely detailed Range Rover and even managed to stain his Off White Air Max's. Priest became so enraged that he slammed on the brakes and threw the truck into park. He grabbed Reena by her collar with such force that his upward motion busted her bottom lip. She began throwing a barrage of windmill punches and Priest exited the car, though not to escape her assault. He darted to the passenger door, wrestled Reena from the truck and threw her to the ground. He then jumped back into his vehicle and drove off. Reena was left on the side of the road with a bloody lip, ripped shirt and a shattered phone screen.

Normally Lock would be her first call, but he was away at school, so Reena called Castle to pick her up. He flew to her location like a banshee. When he saw her there disheveled and beaten, it actually took Reena about an hour to talk him out of retaliating. After driving around for a while and calming each other down, Reena asked to be dropped off at home. As they arrived at her place, Priest was leaving with a bag of clothes. Reena hopped out and began hurling insults at him a mile a minute. Castle jumps from the car and acts as a human wedge between the two combatted lovers. He grabs Reena around the waist and carries her away kicking and screaming. Reena is usually so quiet and subdued that Castle was actually a little frightened. Just then, Priest drops his bag and rushes towards them. However, he's not focused on Reena-he is making a b-line straight to Castle. While Castle still has Reena in his arms, Priest sucker punches him to his right temple. The force of the punch caused Castle to drop Reena and it also spun him around all in one motion. Priest then screamed,

"Why the fuck did you run ya mouth like a little bitch?"

Castle, still trying to gather himself fully and figure out what's going on, put his hands into a fighting guard and replied

"Fuck you, I didn't say shit!"

Castle, being 5'11 and about 170 pounds could have easily backed down from the 6'4, 220-pound figure in his midst, but Castle is all heart. He's not known as a fighter but Salem teaches little boys to be tough and they carry it into adulthood. Castle charged and unloaded a series of rights and lefts. Castle takes advantage of being left-handed which most street fighters can't deal with. He landed a jab and then an overhand left, a shot that would have dropped a lesser fighter, but Priest remained upright. He responded with a right of his own and dropped Castle to the concrete. With blood gushing from his mouth, Castle bounced up no sooner than he hit the ground. He spat out blood in the same fashion a major league batter spits dip at home plate and headed right back in for more. Castle took a few steps and leaped into the air. He faked a kick and, once Priest committed to blocking the kick, threw another overhand left. In mixed-martial arts, they call it a Superman punch. In Salem, it could be called that, but it could also be called getting hit with the Okey-Doke. With Priest being so tall, he never had a Superman thrown at him before so he couldn't properly defend it and the strike landed flush on his chin. He crashed to the earth in mayday fashion. The impact broke Castle's hand and both combining factors ended the exhibition instantly. Reena, screaming for them to stop the entire time, then began to process the origin of the fight and words the two men had exchanged. She turns to Castle with all of her fury and cried,

"You knew, didn't you?"

Castle, still somewhat hunched over and writhing with the pain of a crushed appendage replies, "No, I don't know what you're talking about."

"Then why did he assume it was you that ran your mouth when I never told him who told me?" she iterated.

"I didn't say shit, and I gotta go to the hospital," Castle grits through his teeth.

"Well flame on, and lose my number. Don't call me, and don't come by!" Reena barked angrily.

Normally Castle would have stayed and tried to smooth things over, and tell a self-serving story to get back into Reena's favor, but with a fist made out of shattered china, he decided to head to the hospital and talk it over later. It was never in Castle's DNA to tell Reena, and even though they didn't speak for months and their relationship has never truly been the same, if he had to do it all over again, he would keep his mouth shut the same way. Castle's loyalty to the streets and its codes always seems to go hand in hand with Murphy's Law in relation to his life.

Chapter 3

PROJECT WINDOW

In 1978, a housing community was erected on Salem's eastern-most tip. Whispering Waters Apartments was a quiet neighborhood with 3 playgrounds, two small and one large for kids to enjoy, as well as a recreation area with basketball and tennis courts. Castle moved there when he was 3 years old. His mother was 17 and a senior in high school when Castle was born and this was her first apartment totally on her own. His dad was a 27-year-old hustler who also worked a nice job, drove the finest cars and gave Castle a brother or sister for the next 6 years, none of which were by Castle's mother.

By the time Castle was old enough to ride a bike, the neighborhood had already slipped into the furthest thing from a garden utopia that one could imagine. The place where 20-year-olds with bright eyes and no life experience once co-existed with the middle-aged working class and retirees alike had given way to an open-air drug market where shootings were just background music to the soundtrack of everyday life.

Donovan Castle was infatuated with the street life at an early age. His mother tried her best to keep him away from it, but he still grew up admiring the drug dealers who had money, every pair of Jordan's and all of the prettiest girls. As far as he was concerned, what more was there to ask for? It was a quiet blessing when Castle and Lock became best friends. It provided Castle with some version of a guiding light so that even when he began to stray he would never veer to the point of no return.

Castle sold his first bag at 16 and never looked back. If not for his mother's perseverance, and having a best friend on the straight and narrow, he would have never graduated high school. By then Whispering Waters was nicknamed Iraq Island. Iraq because it was a war zone, and Island because it seemed to be on its own, cast away from the rest of the city. At one point, 40 percent of the violent crimes that occurred in the entire county took place in "Iraq." Eventually, a huge gate was erected, and only residents could enter. The name was changed to Harvest Point in an effort to erase the memory of what had gone on there but everyone still calls it "The Waters." Castle got robbed at gunpoint during the summer before he entered his senior year. It didn't deter him one bit, he just charged it to the game as they say.

Castle endured the valleys and peaks of the drug game. He took his losses, won when he could, and now he's doing OK for himself. He's not rich by any stretch, but he has money in his pocket, the best clothes on his back and a black on black Dodge Charger RT. Life is good! He doesn't sell nickel and dime bags hand to hand anymore-mostly 8 balls, quarter and half ounces. The life always looks better on the outside than it actually is, which is why he was excited when Lock came back to Salem. He looks at the music game as an escape from the streets, but if nothing else it will help him make more money in the streets. To him, it's a win-win situation.

The label that Lock and Castle started really wasn't much of a label at all. It was more like an agreement between two friends. They had very little money, no artists and no music. Castle trusts Lock to the edge of the earth, so when Lock brought the idea to him, Castle was down for it 100 percent even though he couldn't totally see the vision. Lock estimated that they would need about $15,000 to start things the right way. Lock's life savings was a little under $4,000 at that point, but he vowed to save the rest by working extra shifts and weekends at his after school job. He also airbrushed t-shirts and sold as many as he could. Back then, Castle had very little money. He had a few thousand, but he would need that to buy more drugs once he sold what he had. If he gave Lock all of his money, he would have no way to re-up, and it wouldn't be enough anyway. He felt like he only had himself to blame because he was always bragging about how much money he made on the block. Therefor, Lock thought he had way more than he actually did, and was depending on Castle to help get the company started that could change their lives.

Castle made the best decision of his life and his worst mistake ever all in one fell swoop. Feeling backed into a corner he now had to find a way to get the money that he needed for his half of the deal. Even though he didn't have much money, his name was good in the streets. He ultimately settled on asking Attica, a decision that would change his life in ways he has yet to understand.

Castle dealt with Attica many times in the past and it always went smoothly, so Castle figured he had a shot at borrowing the money if he promised to pay it back. He found Attica at his normal location-Union St., better known as U-Block. He laid out his pitch to Attica, asking him for the entire $7,500. He gave his word that he would not only buy all of his drugs from Attica going forward, but he would also work for him to pay it back. Attica almost laughed him off of the street,

"Muthafucka, I wouldn't give my mom seven bands, even if I liked the bitch."

Castle thought "Well, that was pretty harsh." Then he said "Well throw me some work and let me get to it. I got you right back yo, real talk."

Attica was hesitant, and against his better judgment, he decided to front Castle a package. Not because he wanted to help, but he looked at it as a chance to expand his clientele.

"This is what I'll do" he said. "I'll hit you with a point, have my bread and we can go from there."

Castle hid his excitement behind a face of granite as he said "Aight bet" and shook Attila's hand, excited that he now had 4 and a half ounces of coke to flip.

Castle hit the streets immediately. He devised a plan in which he figured could not miss. He would sell the drugs at near wholesale prices, making very little profit. This meant he would get rid of it really quickly, and then he would ask Attica to double the amount. In four days he came back with all of Attica's money, which really impressed him. Castle then asked for 9 ounces but Attica refused, again giving him a "point." Castle applied the same technique, this time making slightly more profit while still only needing 5 days to sell out. His diligence paid off and the next time Attica gave him 9 ounces. A quarter kilo of cocaine. That equals a lot of trust, and if not handled properly could equal certain death.

Castle wanted to move this package as quickly as possible, but he also, having secured a large amount wanted to make as much profit as he possibly could. He sold only a small portion at wholesale. Three weeks later he had all of Attica's money and a nice little profit stacked up for himself. He decided to celebrate a little and grab a hotel room and finally get his hands on a pretty petite chic from Beckett that he had been chasing for a few months. The next morning they go to iHop and then she drops him off back in Salem. Still a little drunk from the high levels of Henny he consumed the night before he gathers up Attica's money and calls him, but the call immediately goes to his voicemail. He calls four more times hoping for it to ring, but to no avail.

He finally decides to head over to U-Block. Before he makes it halfway there he hears the news that has the city on fire. A raid! The task force raided Union Street and Attica was among 7 people arrested. They found drugs, guns and a boatload of paraphernalia. What Castle didn't know at the time was that the warrant stemmed from an aggravated assault charge, and Attica was being held on that as well. With his past record, he was given no bail. Castle had his money but no way to pay him. He thought about giving it to Bad News who was Attica's friend and triggerman, but the idea of giving a cold-blooded killer several thousand dollars in hopes that he would, in turn, give it to its rightful owner didn't seem like a safe bet to Castle. He figured that Bad News would just as likely leave him floating in the river and keep the bread without batting an eye.

Attica would go on to receive a 10-year sentence with a five-year stipulation. About the same time he was being transported from Salem County Jail to Northern State Prison aka gladiator school, Lock was on his way to Atlanta as a freshman at Morehouse. Two separate lives on two very different paths that were now on a collision course that would send shockwaves through this small town like it had never felt.

Months after Lock returns to Salem, still oblivious to the fact that half of his company was funded through money that Castle failed to pay back to a wolf in unmistakable wolf's clothing, his serenity is on track to be aggressively broken. Attica is settling his scores early and will focus his energy on muscling in on the record company that he has heard so much about while locked up. The last of those scores is a trap spot on Sinnickson Street.

Two men sit on a step talking. In New York, they call it a stoop, in the South it's called a porch, but in South Jersey it's called a "step." Anyway, the two men are having a passionate conversation about the recent wave of gunplay that has crashed on the shore of the city.

"I'm just sayin', ain't it a bit funny that everybody who was beefing with Attica is getting killed and this nigga is supposed to be coming home soon?" Moe states while pounding his fist into his palm with each syllable that he speaks.

As this exchange is going on, two other men are standing down the street slightly out of view having a dialogue of their own.

"Here's what I need you to do," News said to Barry.

Barry is one of the local crackheads. He's been getting high since the late 80's and all of the hustlers know him. He constantly brings money to them, but he also comes short a lot. He's always asking to get one for $8 or 2 for 15. Back to the conversation he's having with News.

"Go over there and spend this $100 with them." said News. "I wanna know how they product matches up with ours. You can try to make a deal with them and whatever you get extra you can keep, so try to get like twelve for the buck and you can keep two, just bring me back the 10." News explained.

"I got you," Barry said excitedly. "I'mma see if I can get like 14 of 'em! I bring a lot of money so I hope they look out."

Barry walks over towards Moe and Rock as they sit on the step talking.

"Here come Barry."

Rock replied "I bet you that his ass want a deal. He probably got like $8."

Barry walks up briskly, face beaming with excitement. In a loud and boisterous voice, he says,

"Yo, I got a yard." Yard is South Jersey slang for $100.

"Let me get 14, man. I got a white boy who willin' to spend, but he gotta test it first to make sure it's good. After that he gonna spend man I'm tellin' you, I promise!" Barry proclaimed.

Moe responds "HELL NO! You can't get 14. Take these 12 and get the fuck outta here."

Then Rock chimes in "And you better come straight the fuck back to us when he test it out."

Meanwhile, as this is going on, News has headed in the direction of the 3 men. He is wearing a heavy black coat which is unzipped, a black hoodie and black cargo pants.

His hands are inside the front pocket of the hoodie. He walks with quick steps, but not so quickly as to alarm Rock and Moe. He approaches the 3 men just as the conversation is ending. Without breaking stride he pulls 2 guns from the front hoodie pocket. Both sides of the pocket have slight cuts so that he can pull out quickly without the weapons getting caught. In a split second, he shoots Moe and Rock with the 40 caliber pistol in his left hand. Moe never even sees it, Rock, on the other hand, tries to run after the first shot. He makes it only a step or two before taking 2 slugs- one in the back, and one to the back of the head. Barry is frozen in fear and confusion, trying to process what he just saw. As quickly as News has just executed 2 men in front of him, News swings his right hand in Barry's direction and shoots him twice in the chest and once in the back as Barry at this point tried to turn and run away. His thin frame was no match for 9-millimeter hollow points. As Barry lay quickly dying he clinches the $100 bill that News had given him when they were down the street. News pries the money from his hand ever so quickly and places the 40 cal that he used to shoot Moe and Rock in Barry's hand. He flies over to Moe and places the 9 in Moe's hand. He reaches onto Moe's waist, takes his gun and flees between two houses. The entire ordeal lasts less than 30 seconds.

Chapter 4

NEVER CHANGE

The Walnut Street Field where the Salem Rams play home games is old and run down. The bleachers probably should have been replaced 20 years ago, and the encompassing track is in such disrepair that the once state champion track team can no longer have home meets. Still, this hallowed ground lay claim to some of the greatest sports performances in history. Part truth, part lore, tall tales of Salem-bred giants like Lydell Mitchell, A.B. Brown and most recently Jonathan Taylor will be passed down for generations. In 1988 when Derek White broke the all-time South Jersey rushing record, Robbie Grimes was at every home game. He couldn't afford the $1 admission, so he and a few of his friends snuck in through a hole in the fence behind the concession stand. Robbie was 8 years old when Derek galloped into the history books, and he couldn't wait to get to high school and hear his name called over the loudspeakers as the next great gridiron warrior.

Fate acts only to appease itself and Robbie would never dawn the horns of The Salem Rams. When he was 11, DYFS, New Jersey's child services organization attempted to remove he and his 5-year-old brother from his mother's care. Rather than head to a foster home Robbie ran away. A week later he was caught stealing snacks from Murphy's department store because he hadn't eaten in two days. He was taken to the juvenile detention center, and over the next few years, he would be in and out of custody so many times that he earned the nickname Attica after the New York prison famous for its 1971 riot. When he was 16, he was released from custody and could not wait to get to the block to see what everyone was up to. As he approached, smiling from ear to ear and happy to be free, one of his friends began to chant A-tti-ca, A-ti-ca like the scene from the movie Dog Day Afternoon and the entire crowd found it utterly hilarious. For the rest of the day, his friends all jokingly called him Attica, and his likelihood to be incarcerated just as much as he was free made the name stick.

***

The murders on Sinnickson Street were some of the final pieces to a plan that Attica has been devising while behind bars for the last few years. Just hours after the gunfire, and with the crime scene still teeming with detectives, Attica is a free man.

In the streets it is understood that the less people know, the less they can tell when the cops come knocking. Attica lives by that understanding and navigates in a tight, three-man circle of trust consisting of himself, Bad News and Jason Deloatch, known in the hood as Schemer. With Bad News' hands full committing atrocities on Attica's behalf, it is left to Schemer to receive their newly-freed associate as he walks through the prison gates.

Attica takes his first steps of freedom with a customary fishnet sack containing all of his prison belongings. Waiting by the curb is Schemer in a black late model Toyota Camry. The vehicle is nice, but not so nice that it attracts attention. The only modification is a slight tint added to the back windows. It is illegal in NJ to tint the front driver and passenger windows, so to avoid conflict those two are clear. Schemer reaches down and pulls on the lever that releases the trunk and exits the car. As he rises to full attention he hears Attica say,

"Look at you, all grown now."

He extends his right hand for a shake which is constricted into a customary embrace.

"Welcome home! How are you feeling?"

Noticeably happy, as most would expect in this situation Attica says,

"Like a lion out of the cage... Like a lion out of the cage."

They enter the idling carriage and begin their trek to Salem. With so much to catch up on, the conversation winds like a back road in Virginia. The most pressing matter at hand is discussed almost immediately as Attica asks

"What's up with News?"

Needing no more words to be said, Schemer replies, "He good, it's good. I just talked to him."

This implies that the situation on Sinnickson Street is all taken care of. Since Attica had been going through the process of being released at the same time it was all happening, he didn't have access to a phone for any updates. He also, on his way out, was away from population where news almost always reaches inmates before the masses on the streets because someone is always on a call to home.

When the two men reach Salem, they head straight to Bad News' place. Attica wants to keep it quiet that he is home for at least a while, and he wants to have News and Schemer update him on everything he's missed.

Schemer knocks on the door but never tries the knob or walks directly in. News is quick to the trigger and entering his house unannounced could be a death sentence, even if accidental. After a few short seconds, Bad News answers the door. Schemer walks in, followed by Attica. Following News into the room he states "Look what the wind blew in!"

"Awwww shit! What's up?!" News says to Attica.

The two men shake hands and embrace one another.

Attica growls "My brother! What it do?"

News responds "I'm maintaining. Is this your first stop, or did you go check out Tiff and your son?"

Attica's eyes drop to the floor.

"Nah, I ain't been by there yet. She don't even know that I'm out. She was pretending to hold me down, acting like everything was sweet, but I heard about all of the shit that bitch was doing." Then he pauses for a second as his eyes rise to once again meet News' and he says "Why didn't you tell me?"

With a look of sincerity plastered upon his face News states

"Because it was undue stress. It ain't like you was gonna turn into The Incredible Hulk and bust through those walls, so I felt like it was better to not tell you until you touched down. Trust and believe I planned on letting you know everything, but not while you was already in a cage."

As Attica gives Bad News a fist bump as a goodwill gesture he replies

"I feel you. Good looking out."

With a look as if an idea has just materialized in his head News says

"So what do you want to do about this nigga Tone that she was dealing with?"

Attica prides himself on adherence to the code of the streets. He responds with

"When I see him, if he keep it real everything is fine. If he tries to shake my hand and act like we're cool, well then I'm gonna have to light fire to his ass for trying to play me. He ain't my friend so he don't owe me any loyalty, but the whole world owes me respect. Either pay it to me or I take it!"

As cool as ever, News simply states "I'm with you."

Schemer instantly chimes in

"And I'm with both of y'all but damn, let's go get something to eat. I know you are happy to not be eating state food. What do you want to get first?"

Attica can be quite dramatic at times, he says to Schemer

"I'm hungry for paper. Let's go sit down and plan the next move. What's up with that nigga Castle? Have you seen him?"

Schemer says

"Nigga, not today, but let's talk about it while we eat-I'm hungrier than a muthafucka!"

Attica hasn't had good food in quite some time, so Schemer's proposal sits well with him. They decide to head over the bridge to Delaware. There's a Hooters on Route 13 and Attica loves the Honey Thai wings there.

Once they are seated, it's right back to business.

Attica leans in with his elbows on the table and the weight of his upper body pressing downward.

"I just want to get my head straight before the streets know that I'm home. That's why I ain't wanna to go to none of the places in town. Nobody knows I'm out except for you two."

After digesting that information, News says

"It's a lot different out here since you went down. Coke money dried up. Still money to be made, but not enough for everybody. Either we control it, or it ain't worth it.

Attica's eyebrows raise

"Word? So who out here is getting it like that?"

Schemer jumps in

"Do you remember Remo? Well, his little brother Reggie is rocking and rolling."

Laughing, Attica says "Little Reggie huh?"

News inserts

"When Remo got killed he started

going hard. Got a little crew together. They dropped a couple bodies since you been gone."

Attica begins to shake his head as if things are beginning to become more clear.

"So what else is heavy?" he asks.

News taps two fingers on the table as he says

"I know the pills was around before you left, but not like this. The coke got replaced by these pills. The pill game is where it's at. Young bitches out here fucking for percs like certified crackheads."

"True that." Schemer says "The weed is totally different too. Everything is "loud" now. Regular weed won't sell anymore, only loud. It's going for like 35 to 4 bands a pound. Since the coke money is so slow though, everybody and they Mom is trying to get in the loud lane."

Rubbing his beard with the tips of his fingers Attica replies with

"I'm gonna do the knowledge on the coke thing. We can definitely take that over. If either of you have a connect for the pills, and it's as serious as you say it is, bring it to the table and we can make a run."

He motions to Schemer.

"Did you call Castle again?"

"Yeah. Nobody picked up."

A little agitated, he says

"Are you sure that you have the right number?"

Schemer says with confidence

"Yeah, I sold him a couple of phones about a week ago."

Attica states

"I have some serious business with him. Make sure I speak to him

before the night is out. It could get really ugly for him real fast. It's not a game."

Schemer picks his phone up from the table.

"Word, I'll hit him up again."

Castle has been selectively ignoring his phone all day. He sees the numerous calls
from Schemer, but figures that he probably has more phones to sell so he will call
back later. Like the rest of the town, he has no idea that Attica is now free, which
means he also has no knowledge of the impending hailstorm headed his way.

Money never came in abundance to Attica as a child which caused him to covet it
more once he started to earn. When he was 10 years old, he slept in a bedroom that
had nothing in it but an old box spring and mattress lying on the floor, and an empty
dresser. He had enough clothes to fill only about two of the drawers. He had two
posters on his wall and he would gaze at them each night until he fell asleep
pretending to be his heroes Jerry Rice and Michael Jordan. When he was locked up in
juvie at age 11, the bright spot of his whole stay was when the guard let him stay up
late to watch The Bulls won their first championship. He was so excited that he didn't
sleep that night. He replayed the game in his mind over and over again until daybreak.

He held tight to those rare moments when he could lose himself into a world outside of his own. Sooner or later reality would set in, returning him to a bland existence where his shoes were never new, his clothes were hardly washed and his stomach was seldom full. He learned how to fight as a means to combat those who thought it a good idea to point out that he wore the same jeans on Monday, Wednesday and Friday. There was never much doubt about whether or not Attica would eventually try his hand at the illegal drug trade. He didn't do it to be ostentatious. He knew that it was not a guarantee that he would eat outside of the free lunch the school provided, and that with winter coming, the cardboard on the inside of the sole of his shoe would no longer be a sufficient patch for the hole there upon the first snowfall of the year.

Attica got robbed his first night selling drugs. A stickup kid named Shank strong-armed him. Shank was a 6-foot bruiser, built like Tony Atlas. He used his size to intimidate and extort young dealers. If they didn't give in to his demands, he just took everything. Attica, just a few hours into his inaugural shift as a corner boy comes face to face with Shank. Being so new to the trade, he didn't know that Shank was someone that he should be avoiding at all costs. He approached Attica and said

"Yo, you holdin?"

Attica, as nervous as possible, but faking bravado uttered

"Yeah, what you need?"

Shank asked "What you got?"

Attica responded

"I got dimes."

Shank took a step closer and said

"You know what? Gimme all of that."

By the time Attica realized that he was inside the jaws of a shark, the teeth had already sunk in. He turned to run, but before he could take a step he could no longer breathe. Shank had locked his massive arm around his neck and began carrying him down the street. He whisks Attica into the dark between two houses and demands all of his drugs. Attica bravely refused and Shank literally tore his pockets off, leaving him with nothing. Attica was completely disheartened and vowed to never be so stupid or weak again.

After the incident with Shank, Attica felt like a baby lion forced to hunt for food among fully grown hyenas. As each day passed he learned more, and as he began to grow, so did his boldness. By the time he turned 16, strong-armed robberies were a threat that was in his rear view mirror. His only opposition at that point were shooters and police. There was a rumor once that Attica had given out credit to a smoker who asked for drugs until that Friday when he got his check. When the check came, instead of paying Attica, he bought from another dealer. Attica didn't catch up to him until Sunday, but when he did he was so livid that he threw the smoker into the trunk of his car and drove around with him in there all day. He didn't let him out until the next morning. Attica felt like if people thought he was crazy, then no one would play when it came to his money. Castle knows this story, among others. If he had any idea that the reason Schemer was blowing his phone up derived from Attica chomping at the bit to talk to him, Castle would have answered on the first ring of the first call.

Since Schemer can't get ahold of him by phone, Attica feels that maybe other tactics need to be applied.

Castle walks down the street swinging his arms back and forth as he bops to the beat of the trap music that he is reciting in his head. His cell phone rings and he

ignores it. He has several missed calls from Schemer but doesn't answer this one either. He turns a corner and continues his strut. His phone rings again, he again neglects it. He walks up to his door with a little hop that allows him to skip two of the three steps leading to the entrance. He fumbles around for his keys for a few seconds before finally securing the correct key to unlock the door. While his head is still down, out creeps a figure dressed in all black. He raises a 45 caliber pistol and points it to the back of Castle's head. Just as his head lifts to an upright position, Bad News, the man holding the gun lightly presses the barrel against the base of his skull and calmly says only one word,

"Castle…"

Chapter 5

BLACK GIRL LOST

Salem High School sits on the outskirts of the city's southern border. Years ago, when the funding for bussing dried up, many of the students were left to make the extensive journey on foot. The long strip of pavement that represents the last leg of the daily pilgrimage came to be known as "The Stretch." No one knows exactly how the moniker actually began, but it can possibly be accredited to the way that the sidewalk seems to stretch on forever into the horizon. Reena and Milan have been what one would call friends since they were 10 years old, but nothing galvanized the relationship like their long talks to and from on The Stretch each morning and afternoon.

The dog years as they are sometimes called. The pubescent period often linked to the high school experience where teens undergo huge leaps in maturity, likened to the way dogs age. This time is also associated with retrospective fondness, widely seen as some of the best years that life ever dispenses. For Reena these years were turbulent and Milan, like a faithful first mate, was along for the ride. Reena, in turn, was a constant refuge for Milan.

Freshman year when Reena missed two weeks of school while suffering from vertigo, Milan went to each of her teachers and gathered all of the work Reena missed so that she could maintain her straight A average. In October of their sophomore year, Milan's grandfather had a stroke at the wheel and died a week later. Milan was crushed and Reena just about moved in with her and her mother. For close to the next month Milan cried herself to sleep on Reena's shoulder each night. A year later it was Reena who was in a car accident as a back seat passenger. She wasn't badly hurt, but the impact of her face flying into the headrest gave her a black eye and left her with a chipped front tooth. For Reena, this was a fate worse than death. It would be about a week before the dentist had an opening to fix her tooth and the thought of having to carry on everyday life with a jagged incisor mortified Reena. Lock dropped by to assure her that all would be fine and to remind her of all the great things that both Nas and Fabolous had accomplished with chipped teeth. Reena didn't find an ounce of humor in the gesture. It was Milan who hurried to Reena's side, makeup bag in tow. She did such a number on Reena that aside from a little swelling, the black eye was all but a memory. As for the chipped tooth, Milan purchased Reena a set of fake gold grills from Cowtown, the famous local flea market. It was the only thing that she could think of-besides, it only had to last a few days.

Seven months after "Tooth Gate" as junior year drew to a close, Milan got the shock of her young life. She was pregnant. She had no idea what to do. She didn't tell anyone but Reena and sobbed to her for 8 whole days before finally telling her mother.

A few months or so later, Reena's world would too be turned upside down. Her parents were out of town for a week as the Summer began, and she was completely unsupervised. Normally pretty responsible and a straight-A student, her parents deemed her low risk as far as liabilities go. Without a curfew, she found herself away from home in the middle of the night, and at the crossroads where the wrong place intersects with the wrong time. She was staring down the barrel of a police-issued riot pump.

Reena's scholarship to a prestigious once-in-a-lifetime summer program was immediately rescinded, and all offers from the universities that she had hoped to attend were one by one withdrawn. Needless to say, she was devastated. For a fraction of a second, she even flirted with the idea of jumping to her death from the Delaware Memorial Bridge, but the thought of animals nibbling at her body quickly flushed the thought cleanly away. Lock and Milan played a major part in helping Reena keep it together during senior year. Castle was not too far behind, offering his support and of course his heart if Reena would so kindly oblige.

When Milan's daughter Amara was born, she made Reena the godmother. Despite different upbringings, Reena being from a two-parent household with rules and structure while Milan was raised solely by a mother working too many hours to keep a sufficient eye on her, both grew to look at the other as a sister. However, jealousy would begin to creep in as the two women, both beautiful by all accounts, were constantly viewed in different lights. Reena was coveted as a kind of hood princess. A low-budget Beyoncé with Kelly Rowland's complexion while Milan was the ratchet, light-skinned girl whose hazel-eyed grace often took a back seat to her elevated decibels. For years Milan instantly stamped down any bitterness that would attempt to arise in her mind, but over time a multitude of even the tiniest cracks can crumble the sturdiest of foundations.

When Reena brushed off Milan's pursuit of Lock all of those feelings came rushing in, similar to the last small microfracture needed for a mighty dam to succumb. Like those waters now free to rage, the flow of Milan's raw emotions are headed crashing in Reena's direction. A few hours later she shows up at Reena's house with a plan to secretly drive a wedge between Reena and Lock.

Milan sits down, but no sooner than she is seated she pops up and heads for the bottle of wine that the two drank from earlier.

"Have a drink with me," she yells to Reena in the other room.

"I'm good, I didn't even finish the first glass," she replies.

"Well that's all the more reason to have a drink with me now," Milan demands as she re-enters the room double-fisting the beverages.

She hands Reena a glass, and as she sits down asks

"How much longer till you graduate?"

"Oh god, not for about another year and a half. Seems like forever away."

Sounding upbeat Milan states "Girl, you're almost there. Plus with everything you had to go through to get here, you should be happy."

Reena stares into the glass while gently running her middle finger around the rim.

"I guess I should be happy that I can still end up in a good situation, but I'm always gonna wonder what if. What if I had just went home that night like I planned. I would have never got caught in that raid and I wouldn't have lost my NASA scholarship, or all of my offers."

"Yeah girl, but it's not like you coulda known."

Reena looks up, still yet to take a sip from her glass and says

"I knew that I should have run away from him as fast as I could as soon as I found out what he was involved in. I was young and dumb though, now I'm gonna pay for it for the rest of my life."

Milan assures her

"You are still gonna do big things girl. Anyway, so I met this guy the other day. We supposed to go out, but his cousin is in town with him. Can you go with me and keep him company?"

Reena raises one eyebrow and looks away and says

"Bye girl."

Milan lets her shoulders fall in exasperation and puts on her best pouty face.

"Reena! Please. Come on! He sent me a picture of him and he mad cute. They both get money too girl!"

Rena rolls her eyes and says

"Now you know I don't care about some guy and his money."

Milan shoved her phone in the direction of Reena's face.

"Just come with me please. Here look at him."

She shows Reena a picture on her phone.

Reena twists her lip as if she is giving it some thought.

"He is cute, but I don't know."

Sensing that Reena had already been reeled in, Milan blurts out

"I'm gonna call him and tell them that we can meet them on Friday night."

Still a little hesitant Reena replies

"I didn't say yes."

This agitates Milan and with a hint of aggression she responds with

"What are you scared that Lock is gonna find out? Girl get over it. I really need you. Don't leave me hanging."

"I'll think about it." Reena says.

With total disregard for Reena's apprehension, Milan finishes the text she had been typing, drops her phone into her Prada bag with a flip of her wrist and states, "There's nothing to think about. Just be ready on Friday."

Back as Milan entered the eighth grade, her father achieved a full year disburdened by the crack habit that ravaged him during her earlier years. With a new job and girlfriend, he moved to New Castle, Delaware for a fresh start. Milan spent a few weekends there and was pretty underwhelmed as she mainly sat in the den and watched TV. She wasn't exactly thrilled about spending part of her summer there. She was however stoked at the fact there was a pool she could swim in whenever she pleased. Her dad seemed to be doing a lot better now, but without him around much up to this point she knew her fair share of struggle and she still harbored resentment. On top of that, Milan didn't care one bit for her dad's new girlfriend. Two days after Milan arrived she was asked by the girlfriend to perform a favor. The neighbors had just moved in not long before from Maryland, and they had a daughter Milan's age who could use new braids. Milan was on the precipice of a meltdown when the words "Oh yeah, they said they'll pay you" instantaneously transformed fire and brimstone to a babbling brook.

Milan arrived to perform the service and more importantly get paid. She planned on being cordial but didn't have the energy to lay on a masked cherubic persona. Small talk eventually blossomed into a full-fledged dialogue lasting long after Milan finished the job. She and Monae, the girl whose style she just completed, hit it off quite nicely. They liked the same music and even the same TV shows. They both would have been perfectly fine with wearing purple every day for the rest of their lives and also both wanted to one day play in the WNBA. Maybe Delaware was not so bad after all.

After a few weeks of being fused at the hip, it was time for Milan to head back to New Jersey. The duo would text, send each other messages on MySpace and even video chat on ooVoo whenever the opportunity afforded.

Milan's relationship with her dad did not improve much. He was no longer getting high, but he still hardly ever saw her, and the two never formally buried the hatchet when he first got clean. Milan began to make the trips to Delaware solely to hang out with Monae. By the next summer, she could barely stand to be in the same room as her father's girlfriend and slept at Monae's house on all but one of her nights there. Once school was back in session they begged Monae's parents to let her spend a weekend in New Jersey. After many failed attempts at coercion, Monae was finally given permission.

Monae's first day in Salem was action-packed. Milan took her to all the spots where the guys hung out, knowing that they would all want to know who the pretty little thick jawn was that none of them had seen before. Milan loved the attention, and the buzz around Monae put the spotlight back on her as well. They gave out a few numbers and took a few as well. After hitting the hot spots in town, Milan took Monae to meet Reena. They sat on Reena's step for over an hour, talking about boys and basketball. Reena didn't play basketball like Milan, but she loved Kobe Bryant and The Lakers. Monae, being from Maryland, was a huge Kevin Durant fan with him being from DC. The Thunder months earlier lost to the Lakers in the playoffs and Monae chalked it up to luck. Reena, of course, exalted Kobe to near deity status, and felt that statement was absurd. The boy talk was long gone as three high school girls argued about basketball like their lives depended on it.

When Monae returned home she began to keep in touch with Reena as well, especially when the Thunder played the Lakers. They would go periods of time without speaking but would always pick up right where they left off. Milan, on the other hand, stayed in constant contact with Monae spent the entire summer after graduation in Salem. The town has an unexplainable way to somehow beguile visitors and eventually, Monae moved to town. She went on to have a son by a silver-tongued corner boy who fed her dreams that were part Tony Montana and part Cliff Huxtable. It didn't quite materialize that way so while he is doing a 5 flat in South Woods State Prison, she works in a warehouse full-time and is in training to become a phlebotomist. She hangs out often with Milan and connects with Reena once every blue moon. On rare occasions, all three of them hang out and it is like they are teenagers again.

***

After refusing to take no for an answer on the group date idea, Milan leaves Reena's place happy that her plot is beginning to take form. Before driving off she searches her playlist for the perfect song but decides to call Monae instead. Minutes after putting her son to bed Monae answers the phone delighted to hear from Milan as they haven't spoken in a few days.

"Milly-Rock, what's up girl!?"

"Bitch, what you doing?" Milan replies.

Fighting off a yawn Monae says,

"Nothing, just put the baby to sleep. I'm tired, about to get something to eat."

Yawns seem to be contagious so after hearing Monae yawn Milan begins to yawn as she utters her response.

"Lock is having a party next week, you tryna go?"

Monae starts to mentally go through her previous engagements and says "I'm pretty sure that I don't work next weekend so that's cool."

She then asked Milan

"What you got going on this weekend though?"

She tells Monae

"I'm going out on Friday. I'm double dating with Reena. This dude is lame, but he gets money. His cousin is really cute and I'm trying to hook him up with Reena."

Monae quickly asks,

"Well damn girl if he that cute you shoulda hooked me up?"

Milan opens up a tiny window into her artifice.

"I'm trying to get Reena to like him so she can stop guarding Lock like her damn life depends on it."

Confused, Monae interjects.

"I thought you said that they like, love each other or something like that?"

As she rolls her eyes to the back of her head Milan states,

"I guess. She's on some corny ass Joey Potter shit and I guess Lock is Dawson. What she need to do is stop babysitting and let me have him."

Monae isn't on board with what Milan is saying.

"But y'all are like best friends since forever?"

A little frustrated with Monae's pushback, Milan replies

"Yeah girl, but damn. She don't wanna move out of the way, so I gotta nudge her ass a little bit."

"That is wrong Milan."

In a raised voice Milan barks

"Who's side are you on?"

Monae pleads

"I really like Reena, but I'm not as close to her as I am to you. I'm always on your side, but I'm just saying."

Milan again barks, "What are you saying?!"

Monae utters, "Nothing, just forget it. All I'm saying is that I'm staying out of it. Are you going with me to get my nails done tomorrow?"

Milan agrees and the two hang up their phones, ending the call. This further cements Milan's initiative as she knows that Reena would be by her side for every minute if only they attended the party together. With Monae in the picture, it gives Milan room to operate. Game on.

Chapter 6

COMING OF AGE

According to The Oxford English Dictionary, the word "notorious" is defined as famous or well known, typically for some bad quality or deed. In the 90's, Carpenter Street was by far not only the most notorious street in the city of Salem but the entire area as well. If a person knew only one thing of the city it was to not venture down Carpenter Street. By 1996 when Bad News was a 10-year-old resident of the iniquitous boulevard, cocaine flowed like the Euphrates. The street was so densely covered in broken glass that it looked as if a sequin carpet had been laid. The hustlers stood in small groups and peppered the sidewalk on both sides from end to end. The alleys behind the houses were blockaded with old couches, bike frames, metal dumpsters and anything else that made them undriveable. This prevented sneak attacks from the police. In those days, officers rarely patrolled the area anyway. A few times a week at best.

As a pre-teen, News would sit on his step and watch life play out. He didn't have cable and this was the next best thing. From observation alone, he became an expert on the mechanics of a drug transaction. One day he was offered a job as a lookout. The job paid $20 a night, but he had to be out until daybreak. News didn't care. For the chance to make $20 almost everyday to do something that he did for free? Well, for that he would greet the sun with a smile. As $20 bills began to accumulate, News had more money than he'd ever seen before. He was a have-not, so to be sitting on a few hundred dollars was a big deal to him. He contemplated his next move. He decided that instead of buying his own drugs to sell, he would instead cop a pistol. At 12 years old he acquired a .38 special for $260. He was fascinated by the handgun, sometimes going to his room 10 times a day just to look at it. A month after getting the handgun, he was working his normal post as a lookout when he was approached by a customer that he had seen in the block many times before. It was a quiet night around

3 AM. The customer had a sawed-off shotgun that he wanted to exchange for drugs. News didn't have access to the drugs because he was just a lookout. The shotgun wasn't brand new and the butt had a few chips so, just as he had observed the hustlers do when he watched from the step, he began to negotiate down. The original asking price was $150 but News knew he would never pay that. Having a sawed-off would be nice, but he already had a weapon, and before he overpaid he would just as soon keep his money. He thought about brandishing his gun and just taking the shotgun, but he didn't want to risk losing his job as a lookout for robbing a steady buyer. After a bit of slick talk and threatening to walk away from the deal two times, he bought the gun and a box of shells for $85.

Having two guns and what he considered a pocket full of money made News feel 10 feet tall. Such a young kid, in fact, no one even called him Bad News-yet he was still known as Arthur Bryant or Art for short. He knew that he would make a reputation for himself one day, but his mind was absent the blueprint for just how loudly his name would soon ring bells.

A light drizzle fell on a Sunday evening and News was outside. He wasn't on lookout duty, but he didn't have much of a life besides hanging out. There was a new police officer on the force who was really the gung-ho type. He was beginning to be revered as the cop who would jump out and run down anyone who attempted to flee. He patrolled the area earlier that day and chastised a group standing in front of a house a few doors down from News. He even frisked one of the guys standing there, throwing all of the contents of the man's pockets to the pavement. After his departure, News began to concoct a planned offensive. He placed his shotgun on the side of the house across the street and a few doors down. He changed into an all-black outfit with a black hoodie, which in Salem was not distinctive at all as on any given day close to 100 people could be found dressed in black. He wore a mask around his neck and tucked it into the hoodie.

Hours later when the patrol car began to bend the corner onto Carpenter from Third Street, News retreated between the houses. His tongue instantly became as dry as the desert and began to stick to the roof of his mouth. He noticed a change in his breathing, though he couldn't quite identify what the difference was as he raced to retrieve the firearm. His hands felt as light as feathers and his fingertips were extra sensitive. He rushed to position himself as close to the sidewalk as possible while still being able to remain out of the view of the oncoming service vehicle. He placed the gun behind his back, barrel to the ground so that to a passerby it would look as if he is innocently postured with his hands behind his back. As he heard the engine grow closer his heart began to pound with such fervor that he could hear it inside his ears. His vision was clear but pixelated. Time began to slow down. Just as the car passed he heard the unmistakable squeak that only police brakes seem to make. Before the vehicle could come to a complete stop, he swung the shotgun around his right hip, impeding its flight with his right palm. Without wasting a precious second to aim, he just pointed and fired. A massive boom ripped through the dusk. The flash of muzzle fire momentarily lit the murky walkway as if the sun had been flickered on and off with a light switch. Under siege, the officer fled from what he perceived to be immediate danger which in turn gave News the necessary allotment of time he needed to escape. News could not hear anything other than a steady ring of his eardrums which sounded much like the beginning part of a public service announcement, or when a telephone button is pressed and held down. The smell of gunpowder was from that moment seared into his memory. In under 5 minutes, police were scouring the neighborhood looking for the masked gunman. News could navigate the back alleys behind the houses blindfolded in his sleep and was long gone by first response. Things were so hot that he decided to stay away from the street for about 2 weeks. By that time, he learned that there were no concrete suspects and felt it was safe to come outside. When he finally revealed his face on the block he was already somewhat of a folk hero. Everyone understood what he had done, and they knew that the young boy had heart.

By News' 18th birthday, he was already responsible for several shootings and even two murders. Many of these acts were contracted and occurred outside of the city mainly in Camden and Philly. Out of town shooters are an ideal commodity as they can put in work and disappear without a trace. In the streets, guys like News are called wolves. No successful drug dealer makes it to the top without wolves in his corner. If anyone was ever so lucky to reach the mountaintop without one, they'd be eaten alive in a New York minute. Preme had Prince, Alpo had Wayne Perry and Attica has Bad News. Any cunning leader knows two things: making sure his wolf is fed will prevent that wolf from eating him, and just as importantly it keeps other wolves at bay.

News knows that in a town like Salem, if the murders pile up too quickly or even if dealers go missing in rapid succession the Feds will swoop in and set the whole of the city ablaze, handing out life sentences like watchtowers. He started doing research on the murder rates per capita in an effort to measure the affliction they could impose without garnering federal attention. News isn't the greatest businessman as far as how grams turn into dollars, but in the area of killing and the art of war, he has mastered the science in ways Vivaldi could have only dreamed of mastering strings. Castle doesn't stand a chance against the likes of Bad News. Luckily for Castle, he's more valuable to Attica alive than dead.

Still bathing in the delectation of freshly broken chains, Attica sits with Schemer as he slides through his phone containing pictures of his many conquests whilst Attica was away. Right about that moment the door swings open. Stumbling through the aperture in a manner as if pushed is Castle. His eyes scour the room and upon realizing the figure to his anterior as Attica, he is far more relieved than afraid. Few men have encountered Bad News on a dark street and walked away, so on the entire trip over he weighed the odds of him being killed. The idea that Attica is sitting here coupled with the fact that News hadn't left him slumped in a bloody pile where he found him emboldens Castle just enough that after Attica says,

"My main man, Castle. How is everything?"

Castle responds "Man, what the fuck is all this for?"

Attica replies "Well since you ignored your phone all damn day, I thought to myself, what are the chances that he will just stop by? I figured you needed a little incentive to speed this muthafuckin process up. Nothing like a good ol' gun in the face to get a nigga's feet moving."

While shaking in his boots, Castle put on a brave act and barks

"I don't fuckin know what type of shit y'all are on, but I don't appreciate this shit at all."

Attica grins and extends an open hand

"Calm down, Castle. Is that any way to talk to your business partner?"

Dumbfounded, Castle says

"What the fuck do you mean?"

"I mean that since you started that label of yours with money that you borrowed from me, that makes me an investor, you know, a stockholder." Attica replies.

Castle claps back

"You know damn well that wasn't the agreement we had. I came to pay you back, but you weren't around. Then you got locked up right after that. What the fuck was I supposed to do?"

Sidestepping the previous question Attica says

"So here's the thing Castle. I had a lot of time on my hands, and I took some of that time to study how companies work. Have you ever heard of a valuation? Well, I figure that "our" label is valued at about a million dollars. A modest number as far as I am concerned. All I'm asking is for two-fifty, and I'll be on my way."

Castle, wearing a look on his face as if Attica just asked him the square root of really long number rebuts with

"Two hundred and fifty thousand!? You can't be serious. You know damn well that the label ain't worth that much."

Attica rises to his feet and says

"All I know is that if you know what's good for you, you'll have my bread, or have my seat ready on your board. Come on now Castle, things are looking really good. Let's not turn this pretty possibility into an ugly situation."

Castle, beginning to sulk, says

"I can't believe this shit."

He then turns to walk away and says

"We don't even got a fuckin board."

Attica waves his hand in a shooing motion.

"You can leave now. It would be best if you come find me before I gotta come find you."

Frustrated and dejected, Castle exits the room. In an attempt to get a clearer understanding of what just took place Bad News asks

"So you are really gonna press these dudes for two hundred and fifty bands? We might as well get the slow singing and flower bringing popping, cause ain't no way that they gonna be able to come up with that."

Attica chuckles and says

"I know that they can't come up with that much, that's why I asked for it. We have two possible outcomes. One, let's say they can pull together fifty or sixty bands. I'm willing to take that and walk away. Especially considering the amount that he originally got from me. But what I really want is for them to let me in. That label is headed places, and I'm trying to be along for that ride."

This is music to Schemer's ears and he interjects

"I see where this is going. At this point, killing them is not an option because we wouldn't get shit. What we need to do is put them in a cage, and then just keep rattling it."

Attica says to Schemer

"That's exactly what I was thinking. Make them uncomfortable. Start shattering everything around them. Won't be long before they crack."

Attica along with Bad News and Schemer create a pretty efficient trio. Attica handles the business and News represents the muscle, while Schemer takes care of the intelligence. It's like poetry in motion. Violent, deceptive poetry, but poetry nonetheless. Returning to full strength upon Attica's release brings the winds of change descending upon the city. As the three predators sit in concert, equally deadly in different forms they laugh all but uncontrollably. Reminiscing old stories and treasured moments of hilarity, the lethal potential of one another seems a million miles away. The movies never get that part right. In the streets, the most hardened of killers are the biggest pranksters and wannabe comedians. They laugh and joke constantly. The granite-faced, stiff-postured guys are posers and almost always acting, playing the role that they perceive tough guys to be. The truth is a little less Hollywood while far more complex. Poor neighborhoods are tiny ecosystems, microcosms of the world at large. Lions don't fault other lions for killing gazelles, and guys like Attica don't view the Bad News' of the world as animals for evolving to the top of the food chain in these concrete jungles. The reunited pride is at play, but soon approaches the hour upon which they will look to feast.

Chapter 7

ONE LOVE

On the first Saturday in December each year, the city boasts a tradition. The "Magic of Christmas Parade" marches, motors and plays its way down Broadway. There are local high school bands blaring their best numbers, followed by a line of classic automobiles not too far ahead of a slapstick group of clowns. As traditional Christmas themed floats glide by, candy is flung in every direction as energetic elementary school-aged kids race to secure as many of the fallen confections as their hands and pockets will allow. Vendors patrol each fringe, some with toys and balloons, others with pretzels, hot chocolate or even candy.

For Lock, Reena and Castle the Christmas parade was a sacred perennial event. The tradition began in the 5th grade when they convened across from the corner where Walnut Street flows into Broadway, directly in front of the brick laid church which sits far back from the sidewalk and is besieged by a black steel Victorian gate. Under the gate, every five yards or so lie slabs of limestone that dually acts as bases to sturdy the conduit, as well as decorative accents. The slabs sit in the area of six to eight inches higher than the walkway and allowed Reena to peer above the crowds at the joyous procession each year. Lock grew up on 7th Street, and Reena a stone's throw away on Grant. For those two, the location was a short walk ending rather abruptly after reaching Broadway. For Castle, who lived in The Waters, the rendezvous point was a bit of a hike. This is quite symbolic of their three pointed relationship where Castle has to exert more effort to accompany Lock and Reena in a space that they seem to already occupy. This reality isn't forced, nor has it ever been articulated by any of the three, yet in some way, it is subconsciously understood.

***

After his forced meeting with Attica, Castle is a jumble of nerves. He calls Reena and is denied by her voicemail without so much as one ring. He can't talk to Lock about this, at least not yet, so he heads to Sunoco to buy a pack of cigarettes. He doesn't normally smoke but this is crisis level. With his hands shaking to a near vibration, barely able to spark the end of the cigarette, he wastes four matches before finally finding success. He walks home staring at his feet as they take turns hitting the pavement. Once inside, Castle can't force himself to sit down and constantly paces the living room. Hours elapse and he finally drops to his bed in the loose-limbed manner a rag doll would. The hundreds of thoughts careening through his mind are deafening. He lay still, tirelessly dodging the traffic of his imagination. As night relents to day Castle hasn't slept a wink. He scrolls through his phone for about 20 minutes then decides to get dressed for the day. He showers in silence, something he hasn't done since he was maybe 9 years old. A small act of therapy as the near scalding hot water pounds his head, neck and shoulders. The liquid drumming is a tune all its own. Castle imagines that the multitude of drops are somehow washing his problems away. He exits feeling not much better and he doesn't have anything even resembling a plan. He decides to get dressed and head over to Reena's. Since he can't yet bring this to Lock, she is the only other option.

Castle texts Reena and makes his way to the door. He doubles back to grab his gun which was lying under a pillow on his bed. He ejects the clip and checks the chamber, he then returns the clip and makes sure that the safety is not on. As he reaches for the knob an onslaught of scenarios rush in and he pauses. He gives himself a second to plan an escape should an attack rain down. He thinks of the angles, and which direction to go corresponding with each possible invasion. He then opens the door and steps into vulnerability. His eyes survey the terrain in ways they never have before. He always prides himself on being aware of his surroundings, but this is a far greater representation of that skill. With a brisk pace, he makes his way to his car. Normally he would browse for a song to play, however not today. Sitting still he would feel like a sitting duck. In times of war, a parked car can quickly turn into a four-wheeled sarcophagus. He dives into the driver's seat, puts the key into the ignition as fast as humanly possible and drives away.

When Castle gets to Reena's house, she's not there nor has she responded to his text. He sends her a bunch of frowning face emojis and a gif that says "Waiting." He decides to keep moving and will double back to see Reena once he hears from her. No better place to go than to check up on the people he has fronted packages to. As he's pulling away from Reena's he calls Lock. The phone barely rings before Lock picks up and says

"Hello"

"Yo, what's up bro?" Castle asks.

Lock replies "Nothing, I'm chillin. Busting moves all day. What's up with you?"

Castle asks "Yo, you know where Reena is?"

Lock says "Yeah, she had to meet with her professor. She should be back in town soon."

"Oh, word. I just left her house and nobody answered the door so I was wondering." Castle states.

Lock replies "Word bro, I gotta go, but remember we got that meeting tomorrow. I'll hit you up later to make sure you remember."

Castle agrees and the call is ended.

When Castle arrives on the set he sees Rob who has been a consistent mover of consignment packages. Normally subdued, Castle approaches aggressively.

"Yo, what's up? You got my money?"

Rob replies "Not quite, but I'll have it for you by later today. Tomorrow morning at the latest."

Rob and Castle have had these conversations many times so he did not expect for Castle to pull out a gun and shove it against his rib cage. While grabbing Rob by the collar and shaking him back and forth, still shoving the barrel of the gun as far into his stomach as possible Castle asks

"Are you tryna play me? Huh?"

Totally shocked, Rob says "Yo Castle man, what the fuck? Don't I always pay you? I ain't never short."

Castle begins to walk away and puts the gun back into his waistband. He turns back slightly without breaking stride and says

"Just have my money when I get back. No more of that soft shit."

As Castle drives away he feels totally unhinged. He thinks if he doesn't pull it together soon something bad will happen. He then begins to think in a different light. There's no way he'd be in danger so fast. If Attica kills him, then he won't be able to pay. This point of view relaxes Castle a smidge, and he even manages to grab a bite to eat before checking on a few more people and heading over to Reena's.

Reena answers the door and instructs Castle to follow her to the kitchen. She continues to piddle around as she searches for the components of a quick meal in which she could piece together. Her back is turned to Castle, and while standing on her toes looking into an open cabinet she says

"Sorry for not calling you back. After I left the school my mom called me. You know she talked my head off the whole ride, right?"

The two share a quick giggle and Reena continues.

"I knew you were gonna come back through, though."

With Reena's back facing him, Castle slips into a zone as he admires her hourglass figure, which is accentuated as she reaches for an item just out of reach on the top shelf. He is so spellbound he fails to offer help. She finally manages to tip the can off of the shelf, and as she turns he catches a glimpse of her big brown eye past the partial blockage of hair cascading down from her slightly messy bun. As her spiral continues, Castle is keyed in on her face. Her eyes are two pools-they sparkle with the brightness of an exploding supernova, protected by swooping lashes. Skin of uninterrupted chocolate, her lips are full and her cheeks begin to dimple even at the slightest grin. She has been talking the whole time and Castle has not heard one word. He snaps out of it just in time to utter "That's crazy" as if he was paying perfect attention to the discussion.

The discourse continues, winding into topics far from that of the beginning dialogue. At one point the Loch Ness Monster is discussed, then a rift over whether or not black and white are colors. Castle arrived intent on venting to Reena about his situation, but the conversation is going so well that he doesn't want to ruin it. They haven't talked like this since before the night he fought her ex-boyfriend. It is a moment of clairvoyance for Reena also as she begins to view Castle in a new hue. She instantaneously lets go of the hurt she had been harboring since that night. Her shoulders immediately feel a little lighter, and as Castle is going on and on about whether or not Jimmy Neutron is smarter than Dexter, she is momentarily locked in a doe-eyed gaze and questions why she never gave him a chance.

Over four hours later, Castle decides that he should be on his way. He has business to take care of and Reena agrees that she needs to study, then prepare for work in the morning. As Castle leaves he is floating on cloud nine. He has no idea of Reena's thoughts but he can clearly feel the change of energy and is at least happy to have his friend back completely. His time at Reena's felt so good that he ignored a slew of phone calls and texts so he goes to the block to hang out and also to check on a few people. After arriving, he sees Dame across the street and ventures over to talk to him.

"Yo, what's up? Are you finished with that jawn yet?"

Dame sticks out his hand for a shake.

"Nah, not yet. Almost though. I still got a few left. It's slow out here right now."

Castle responds "You gotta stay dedicated. Sun up to sundown till you get that clientele up. No need to be out here halfway. Either all in, or go get a job and good luck finding one of them."

The entire time Dame is nodding in agreement.

"I feel you. I'm on it though. You gonna see. I'm about to bring you a lot of bread."

"Get it together." Castle replies. "Once you start coming consistently, I'll start hitting you off. Whatever you cop I'll throw you. You gotta prove you can handle it though."

Castle's phone rings. On the other end is Lock reminding him of the meeting that they have scheduled for tomorrow. Lock has been busy taking the advice given to him by Scott Campbell. He has been combing the entire area looking for the right artist. A few with potential popped up in Philly, Delaware and Paulsboro. He put a ton of effort into finding a producer. He wants to bring on an in-house beat maker to cultivate the sound of the label going forward. Once those two things are securely in place, the next step will be to scout locations for a studio. Lock feels like things are moving in a great direction. On top of everything, he has been able to work wonders with his grandfather. In the months that Lock has been back in Salem, he seems a lot better. He eats more and has even gotten invested in a few new shows on TV. He doesn't get around well, but Lock has no problem doing things for him. He feels like one of the last ways to show respect for his mom is to do right by her dad.

Even in his grandfather's hobbled condition, Lock views him in awe. Made of iron and forged in fire. He was born in the Jim Crow South and moved to New York City as a toddler. His entire family was forced to flee after his uncle, who was Lock's great-great uncle, was lynched by the Klu Klux Klan for failing to step off of the sidewalk when a white couple walked by him. The next night, the family's house was burned to the ground, presumably with them inside. However, by the time the embers glowed his family was somewhere in the area of Elkton, Maryland and more than halfway to their metropolitan destination. Lock's grandfather left home at 15 and got a job as a busboy in Atlantic City. The summer after his landing there he met the girl who would become Lock's grandmother on Chicken Bone Beach, the area designated for blacks due to the beaches being segregated in those days. She was there with her family for the weekend and he followed her around like a lost puppy. Finally, just before she left for home he convinced her into providing him with her address so that he may write to her. He penned two letters a week for the next year. Her family couldn't afford to make the trip to Atlantic City the following summer, so Lock's grandfather caught buses and hitchhiked to Salem where Lock's grandmother had lived. He took odd jobs and the pay was not much more than the cost of the room he rented in the attic of a nice old widow for whom he had done yard work. After turning 18 he landed a great position at a small flooring company just outside of town. After a long courtship, and Lock's grandmother's graduation from high school, the two were married in a small ceremony in her parent's backyard. The next year he was off to serve in Vietnam, leaving behind a pregnant wife with the paint on their white picket fence dream yet to dry. He was halfway around the world when Lock's mother was born and would not lay eyes on his daughter until months after her second birthday. Lock knows these stories well. He has heard them countless times growing up. His grandfather is now just a shell of his once mighty self, but all Lock sees is Superman.

Chapter 8

SAY HELLO

There is a bodega-style store nuzzled near the center of Salem. A corner store not quite located on any corner. Travel to anywhere USA and there is a small store or privately owned shop, but for those who have grown up in Salem, New Jersey this particular store is a gem. It is located on the main route to and from school, so many kids meet there for candy and donuts before school or snacks on the way home. Some spent countless childhood hours mulling over comic books there, while adults hustle in and out securing Pick 3 and Pick 6 tickets. The store has changed ownership a few times but for the people of the city, the name stays the same. Anyone from Salem who is old enough to talk and formulate a sentence can provide pinpoint directions as to where "Hank's" is located. The funny thing is that it hasn't actually been named Hank's since around the 1950's when a man of that name owned the locale. Countless people have come and gone, lived and died without ever acknowledging the legal name at any particular time of the landmark.

For anyone Gen Y or later, an actual man named Hank is more believably a wise tale or an urban legend. Regardless of the designation, the market enjoys high traffic all times of day. There's an old local joke that says if looking for someone in Salem, don't venture out-just stand in from of Hank's long enough and they will appear. All jokes contain truth and many encounters occur where the door swings open and shut. Friends have met, fights have occurred and passing greetings must number in the millions. Attica, like most in Salem, has been running in and out of Hank's since childhood. He has brushed past people entering or leaving the store numerous times. No chance meeting more life-altering has ever taken place at that threshold than when he opens the door and standing at the other side is a man named Tone. They are in no way consorts, yet linked in other ways.

"What's up Attica? How are you? When did you get out?"

"I'm good. I just touched down the other day." Attica states.

Through a noticeably contrived smile Tone says to Attica

"Well look my nigga, I'm happy to see you home. You know I fuck with you heavy so if you need anything come holler at me. I got you. You know we go way back bro."

This infuriates Attica and he begins to wear outward notifications as his nostrils flare, but quickly calms himself.

"Word. I appreciate that. What's ya number?"

Attica hands Tone his phone, and Tone puts his number in and passes the device back to Attica.

"I'll be getting with you, most definitely." Attica claims.

Just as he begins to walk away Tone reaches for Attica's hand to shake it, then pulling Attica into an embrace. Attica then walks into the store. He is so irate that he forgets many of the items he came to purchase. He gets into the waiting car with Bad News at the wheel and Schemer in the back seat.

With his eyes fixated forward, in a very calm voice he states

"Get that nigga out of here."

Just as cold, as if a decision of life and death had not just been doled out, Bad News responds

"Say no more."

Expounding upon his rage and disbelief, Attica states

"I can't believe this nigga! Talking about how much he fuck with me, and that we go way back and shit. Then I go to walk away and this muthafucka all but grabs my hand to shake it. It's a wrap for him. I started to give it to him right there. I can't stand when niggas be on that snake shit."

Ever the opportunist, Schemer pleads

"Let me handle it. I will set it up real clean. News you can take it from there. I have a plan."

After putting the vehicle into drive and pulling away News responds "Cool, just make it happen. I'll be ready."

Attica is so livid that he changes his plans and decides to head to the gym. After dropping Attica off, News and Schemer tour through the city discussing matters of utmost importance like what parts of Blac Chyna's body are real, and which was the better show, Martin of The Fresh Prince. News' phone rings and after a few seconds of fumbling it around he finally answers it. The call lasts no more than 10 seconds then he hangs up.

"Yo, I gotta shoot outta town real quick, you tryna roll with me?" News asks.

"No doubt, let's go." Schemer replies.

"What happened to your boy from Bridgeton that said he had those counterfeit bills for us?"

Schemer replies "He's on deck. We can go pick it up now if you want to. If not, we can probably swing out that way tomorrow."

"Nah, not today. We gotta hit CMD real quick."

With an ounce of hesitation, Schemer asks "Why are we going to Camden?"

News says "I have some business up there. Nothing too serious though, in and out."

For Bad News, Camden is a trip that he makes often. Schemer, on the other hand, would rather stay away. Many times, Camden has been rated the most dangerous city in America and not the most welcoming place to strangers. Schemer has been to Camden many times, but it's not a place where he will ever feel comfortable. He does, however, love the food there, especially panzerottis, which are a deep-fried masterpiece similar to a calzone, and stuffed with choice meats. Since Bad News is dragging him to the gates of hell, the least he can do is pay for Schemer's panzerotti.

As they barrel down the highway, going over business opportunities, Schemer asks

"Yo bruh, Attica is trippin' since he got home, right?"

News lets out a short breathy laugh and says

"It's like that sometimes. You don't know how to feel. You hit the block and everybody be showing you mad love, but when you get locked up it's like muthafuckas forget about you. That's why niggas be coming home on some fuck the world type shit."

Schemer takes a second to digest those words, then asks

"Don't you think it's crazy that he ain't try to fuck not one bitch yet? Nigga, I woulda had a bitch pick me up, and I woulda hit they shit immediately."

News responds "He said he ain't gonna fuck with no chics from before he went in. He said he'd rather hold out for something new."

Schemer nods in agreement "Oh, I feel you. I can get with that. But yo, did you ever put Little E in touch with the boy from Paulsboro we talked to a couple weeks ago?"

News wrinkles his brow as if he can't remember, but then it hits him. "Oh, yeah, I did. I took him up there last week. I figured it's better to let Little E do it without me since I'm in Paulsboro from time to time."

"Who did he want clipped?" Schemer asks.

"Some dude named Andre, I guess they call him Dreezy. He showed up on a discovery."

A "discovery" is short for a discovery package. When someone is charged with a crime, the state has to provide the accused's lawyer with the evidence against him or her. Often times including the names of informants.

"Oh word? Who did he snitch on?" Schemer asks.

News answers "The boy that you plugged me in with, his name is Smoke, right? It was his cousin that got snitched on. See, what happens is, they usually give you the discovery but the informant's name will be redacted. Most people cop a plea and it's over. Once you take it to trial, they gotta un-redact the names. He took it to trial and they smoked his boots."

Schemer replies "Damn. Well yeah, that nigga gotta go."

"Yeah bro, real talk. I woulda just did it myself, but I don't wanna keep catching bodies out there. It's too many pretty ass bitches from Paulsboro and if I keep putting in work out there I won't be able to slide." News proclaims.

Schemer wags his finger and says "Yeah, it's definitely a lot of them out there."

News quickly inserts

"Yeah, but my boy lives out there and he always tells me not to fuck with them. Everyone I bring up in conversation, he shoots it straight down."

True to his word, News' dealings in Camden do not take long. Nor does it take long for Schemer to scarf down two panzerottis. He had News buy him four, but he is saving the other two for later. In no time they are back in Salem, and Schemer parts ways with News who is about to go meet up with Attica.

Tone and a few others are carrying out their normal routine. They hang out most days and try to make money while discussing sports and music all day.

"You're crazy! I'm taking Allen Iverson before Isaiah Thomas or Russell Westbrook." Shawn says.

Key chimes in "I'm taking Zeke."

Tone throws his hands in the air with disbelief. Man, what the fuck are y'all niggas talking bout? Give me Westbrook any day. I don't care what neither one of you niggas say."

Just then shots can be heard in the distance.

"Oh shit! Somebody is out there getting busy. Are you strapped up?" Tone asks.

"Is a pig's ass pork?" Shawn replies.

About 10 minutes or so later, as Tone and his friends are still debating, they are approached by Little E.

"Yo, do you know who that was that just took all of them shots at Schemer?" Little E asks.

Tone answers "Nah, we heard the shots but that's it. Anybody get hit?"

Little E responds "I don't think so, but whoever it was damn sure wasn't playing. I'mma holler at ya'll later though."

Tone shakes his hand as he begins to walk away.

"Alright, word we're good then."

He then jumps right back into debate mode.

"So anyway man, if Brandon Roy didn't get hurt he would be top 5 in the league right now."

Schemer is poised between two houses waiting patiently for Tone to part ways with his concert. Once the men finally shake hands and begin to head in different directions Schemer starts to prepare. He darts from in between the two structures and runs directly into Tone. Breathing heavy and acting erratically, he says

"Tone, let me talk to you real quick!"

Shocked by the intensity in Schemer's voice, he replies,

"What's up?"

Schemer grabs him tightly by the arm.

"Attica is tripping man. He sent Bad News out to kill you. I guess he ran into you at the store or something and whatever you said got him pissed the fuck off. I told him not to trip over that bitch and he flipped out on me. News just tried to kill me. He just let a whole clip off at me, he was tryna take my fucking head off."

Tones jaw hits the floor.

"Oh word!?"

While tapping the back of his hand repeatedly against Tone's chest and shoulder he says

"If he's willing to kill me, imagine what hell he'll do to you. Listen, I already called my cousin from Camden. He should down here with one of his shooters in a minute. I told them I would supply the guns, but we gotta pay them too. They want three racks to take out News and Attica."

Tone twists his lip and says

"Three bands though?"

Schemer sucks his teeth and replies

"Nigga, a small price to pay to save your fucking life. I already got the guns, and I got half of the bread. All I need is fifteen-hundred from you and we'll be good. If you don't help me I'm gonna die, and so will you. I got the guns right here. They ain't loaded though. Cousin or not, I ain't handing them niggas loaded guns."

Tone yells in disbelief

"Aw man. What the fuck!"

Schemer begins walking and says to Tone

"Come on, grab up your half of the money. They're already on their way."

Tone takes a couple of quick strides to catch up

"Alright man, come on."

They hurry to Tone's house so that he can retrieve the money. Schemer stays out front typing feverishly into his phone. As Tone exits the domicile Schemer encourages him to hurry. Time is of the essence.

He tells Tone

"I gave them this address to meet us at, that way nobody'll see them or see us talking to them. We can't have this shit coming back on us in no way, shape, form or fashion."

Schemer hands Tone a black book bag.

"Here, you can hold the guns, we can just sit them on the floor and let them sort that shit out. Give me the money so that I can give it all to him at once."

Tone hands Schemer his half of the currency just as they approach their destination. The home looks unlived in. The drapes look old and there are no cars out front. This doesn't seem alarming to Tone-illegal activities are frequently done in dark spaces.

They get into the house and the living room is completely empty. It smells as if rainwater had breached the roof, but had since dried. Tiny chips of drywall crackle under their feet with each step as they make their way through to the kitchen. As they creep past the narrow walkway which connects the main room to the kitchen a figure stands before them. It takes a few more steps before the next person enters the sight line and then finally, once completely into the room, a man sits far to the left on top of the countertop. Tone's mind is racing and he begins to recognize who is in the room. Dollar, Little E, and the figure perched on the stove, the Jersey Devil himself, Bad News. Tone's heart drops to the floor, and he becomes lightheaded. He is realizing that he has been set up. He places his hand on the wall and leans on it like a crutch.

"I shoulda never trusted a nigga named Schemer." he utters.

He is visibly terrified and begins to plead for his life.

"Come on News, don't kill me. Please man. I have kids bro. You know I don't deserve this shit, man. Please."

New jumps down from the countertop and assures Tone

"I ain't gonna kill you dude. Relax."

That instant, a look of relief rushes over Tone's face.

"Thanks News. Thanks man." Tone repeatedly proclaims.

News then interjects

"I'm just here to make sure that you die." and he begins to walk away.

Schemer and News make their way into the living room. Tone continues begging to be spared. He views these attempts as futile and attempts to run for the back door. He takes one step and before his next foot touches the floor he is cut down like a blade of grass. The shots ring out in an initial quick spurt totaling 6 or 7 shots with two separate sounds. After a quick pause, a steady hail gunfire ensues. When the silence returns over 30 bullets have been pumped in Tone's direction and he lay face down, motionless except for a couple of faint struggles at breath. Dollar and Little E having never said a word, leave the room quickly, but only to avoid stepping into the pool of blood rapidly escaping out onto the floor.

After calmly fleeing the scene, News asks Schemer

"How'd you get this guy to just walk right in there?"

Schemer finds this absolutely hilarious and begins to tell News the story.

"So I hit up Little E and Dollar, I told them that I needed them to do something for me. I told Dollar to go into the alley and let off about eight shots, and for him to do it and get the hell out of there fast. Then I told Little E, to go around and ask everybody he saw if they knew who it was that took all of them shots at me. Then I let them know that I would hit them up later on the burn out with a code on where to meet me at. I told him that I called Attica's baby mom a bitch and that he sent you to kill me. The shots that rang out before that was just part of the plan to make my story believable. Easy peasy."

In his explanation, Schemer made no mention of the money that he got from Tone. He has tricked a man into paying to be walked down the green mile.

Chapter 9

CHERRY WINE

There is an old cemetery located at York Street on the east side of the city. Not many, if any, new burials occur there these days. Two huge stone pillars mark the entrance, connected by a high metal arch which reads "Baptist Cemetery." The markers vary from un-carved rock to 20-foot monuments. Foot travelers sometimes pass through as a shortcut to or from The Waters. En route to visit Castle, oftentimes Lock would do just that. He never stopped to look at anything, and seldom did he ever even glance at any of the names of the departed. He almost broke stride once as he gazed at a memorial stretching into the sky much higher than he stood. Not once did it cross his mind that the people lying in his path were once alive and real, with real personalities, real emotions, and dreams for how their lives would turn out. It was not an act of callousness, it just truly never crossed his mind. Lock made numerous journeys through the burial ground, never with knowledge of the largely uncelebrated greatness that lay at his feet. A modest gray headstone baring nothing more than a name, underscored by two separate years representing birth and death, divided by a short horizontal line. Resting there in the ground, as noted by the inscription, is Leon Goslin who went by the nickname "Goose."

Born in Salem in the early 1900's, Goose left home as a teenager to play semi-pro baseball for a small east coast circuit. From these humble beginnings, he would go on to play 17 major league seasons, gathering 37 hits in five World Series appearances while being crowned champion twice. He once won the American League batting crown, and another year he led the league in RBI's. When this son of Salem wrapped up his Major League Baseball career he tallied 2,735 career hits and is enshrined in Cooperstown as a member of the Hall of Fame. Lock grew up loving football and basketball, but the first game that he ever fell in love with was the game of baseball. He started out playing tee ball at age 7 and still loves the game to this day. Resting peacefully just feet from where Lock often tread was a man that he would have viewed as a god. He reached adulthood having never heard the name Goose Goslin, not in school or even in the many little league and senior league organizations that he played for.

When Lock was 12 he was in the middle of an all-star season at 3rd base when due to team needs he was switched to shortstop. He took to the position really well and even liked that often times the throw to first was shorter. He also got to cover second base at times and attempt to turn double plays. One game, like normal, Lock stood hunched in a readied position, hand and glove gently resting on his knees. He always paid close attention to the pitcher as he got into his wind up. This was because his coach instructed him to take small steps forward as the ball reached the plate. This would mean that in the event that a ball was hit in his direction he would already be in motion which would save precious seconds reaching a ball. As the pitch whistled towards home plate, Lock timed his motions perfectly as a routine ground ball was hit his way. He charged to retrieve it and just as he placed the web of his glove to the ground, the ball reached the edge of the infield grass which caused it to pop up like a threatened snake and bite Lock in the face. The initial force knocked him to the ground but not before flinging his glove free from his left hand. Never one to be viewed as soft, Lock hopped to his feet immediately. His coaches, already rushing in his direction motioned for him to lay back down. As he folded back to the ground his left eye and nose were totally numb. He glanced at his hands as he removed them from covering his face to see a small amount of blood. He assured the nervous group of players and coaches surrounding him that he was fine and made his way to the dugout. He was not allowed to continue playing but insisted on staying at the game. Reena hardly ever attended any of his baseball games, maybe three or four during his whole career but she was there to see him go down like Joe Frazier in '73. Castle played a later game and had not arrived to witness it. Other than a black eye, sore nose and swollen cheek, Lock walked away fine, except for the hundreds of times that Reena has brought up the incident since then. She gets a kick out of telling the story and Castle always laughs uncontrollably while wishing that he was there.

***

Lock is in awesome spirits as he prepares for his meeting with Castle. He is blaring music while he irons his clothes, yelling out lyrics with perfect timing matching the artist on the song. He two-steps from one side of the ironing board to the other with the energy of a toddler. He feels like his life is in an upward swing, and he has also secretly decided to go out on a limb and take chances that he never would before.

After steaming his outfit to perfection he goes into the bathroom to brush his teeth and tend to his hair. As he reaches for his toothbrush, he catches a glimpse of himself in the mirror which causes him to look deeper. "Am I too skinny?" he thinks to himself. The doubt crept into his head based on a conversation he had with a very attractive female roughly four or five days ago. She told Lock that in the exact same fashion guys are attracted to girls who are considered "thick," females prefer that men have meat on their bones and are not rail thin. For Lock who stands 5 feet 10 inches tall and weighs 164 pounds, he's definitely thin. The only thing that saves him is the naturally muscular build to his slim frame. His shoulders are broad and his pecks show promise. The ink sprawling across his chest reads "Heavy Lies The Crown." He has the arms of a man who is 15 pounds heavier, both of them not completely covered but heavily tattooed. He starts to brush his teeth but then stops briefly to slick his dense eyebrows with his finger. He stares at the mirror into the corners of his eyes to make certain no coal is present. His eyes aren't hazel, but still an abnormal shade of brown. Enough of a difference that he is asked occasionally if he wears contacts. His nose is semi-broad and round. It bares the scar of a nasty tumble that he took when he was seven years old. The mark is no longer visible, but Lock can still feel the slight indentation as he runs his finger down the bridge and to the base of his nose. His mustache and chin hair don't quite connect to make a full goatee, and the rest of his face is absent of any growth. His light brown skin carries few blemishes and an even tone. His hair is soft and kinky, tapered to a fade on each side and rising otherwise close to an inch above his head.

After scanning himself thoroughly, Lock gets dressed and hurries to the eatery where the meeting will be taking place. In true Lock fashion, he is 45 minutes early and he never sits with his back to the door. He goes over his notes and then scrolls through all of his social media accounts. He shoots a couple of shots on Snapchat before next sending two emails. No sooner than that Castle arrives. Lock cheerfully rises to his feet in an effort to greet his lifelong friend and immediately recognizes the subdued demeanor that drapes Castle.

"Yo bro. Everything alright?"

Castle bites his bottom lip, takes a noticeable in-breath and replies

"Yeah, I'm straight bro. So what's on the agenda?"

Lock leans forward and says

"So, I might have an artist for us to sign, and a producer!"

Castle a bit perplexed asks

"Really, from where?"

Lock looks even more excited to answer the new question and he states

"The producer is from Woodbury, but the rapper is from Salem! Mellina's little brother. Mellina that went to school with us. You might not remember him 'cause he didn't come to high school till after we graduated. But they should both be on their way here now."

Squinting his eyes and looking toward the ceiling, Castle asks

"So what are we gonna offer then? How can we get them to sign?"

Lock sits back and extends his arm out to rest on the table.

"Just gonna keep it real with them. No money up front, but it ain't like they're out here making money yet anyway. I think we should just offer them a bigger piece on the back end and promise to go as hard as possible."

Castle totally agrees, but his mind is clouded by the secret he is holding onto. He nods a yes, then Lock says to him

"Oh yeah, and I'm thinking, if we can make it happen with both of them, then it's time to get a studio popping. I'm probably gonna check a few spots in the next few days."

They go over plans for the next few minutes. The artist arrives and sits down next to Castle. Lock then requests that Castle sit next to him so that they can both face him while they speak. Once the seating arrangements have been sorted he introduces the two.

"Castle this is Damani, and Damani this is Donovan, we all call him Castle though."

Castle interjects

"Yeah, I know him. We never really talked, but I know you. I was in the same grade as your sister. I remember when she used to walk you to school."

Lock steps in to bring Castle up to speed.

"So Furious Stylez is his rap name, and here are the numbers."

He slides a piece of paper over to Castle with the number of followers that Stylez has on each social media platform.

He turns his attention back to Stylez and he leans forward with focus. In a moment of extreme honesty, he says.

"Look bro, I'mma keep it real with you. I usually throw on a proper voice and lay things out nice and pretty. Now I'm not saying that you don't deserve that, but I look at it like this-we're both from the same hood, so I'm just gonna give it to you straight. We want you to sign with us, and we'll do everything to get you buzzing. We got a lot of stuff in play, and it's definitely gonna get greater later. Now what do you feel like you need from us?"

Stylez takes a second to gather his thoughts and then responds

"I really just need somebody in my corner. I got everything else. I can make tracks that dump, but I need to get on the radio and stuff like that."

Castle's phone pings as a text message from Reena comes through that reads

"Wyd?"

Castle types back

"Chillin. Sup?"

As Castle places his phone back on the table, Lock promises Stylez that he and Castle are the best place for him. They go over various details for the next 30 minutes before Lock even realizes that the producer hasn't shown up. He sends him a text message but doesn't get a response. Finally, Lock invites Stylez to the party he is throwing, which will give Stylez an idea of the events that can be put together. The three men shake hands and prepare to exit. As Stylez begins to leave, Lock blocks Castle's path with his arm and then sits back down. Next, he says to Castle

"Sit down for a second, I wanna talk to you."

Castle immediately questions whether or not Lock has heard anything about the situation with Attica. Even though his mind is moving frantically, he calmly states

"What's good bro? What you wanna talk about?"

Lock looks downward as he begins to speak,

"So I was thinking. I kinda feel like I've been playing shit too safe my whole life. I let a lotta stuff slip by."

Castle's phone pings again, and again it is Reena.

"Wya?"

He responds

"Be there in a min. Want me to bring anything?"

As he ends the text, he says to Lock

"I mean so, what do you mean? Like, what are you tryna say?"

Another message from Reena comes through almost immediately.

"No. Just hurry up. I want to talk to you."

Castle types

"Ok, be omw soon."

Lock begins to explain

"So.... You remember Chrissy?"

Wearing a resting face, Castle answers

"Yeah."

Lock then states

"Back when I first"...

Castle immediately cuts him off

"Dog, it's a million fucking Chrissy's out here. How am I supposed to know which one you're talking about?"

"Whatever man" Lock replies.

"Mixed Chrissy that used to live on Johnson Street."

While trying to jog his memory, Castle asks

"I think I know who you're talking about. What's her last name?"

Lock says to him

"Her last name is Eves. You know who I'm talking about, her dad is white and her mom is black. Remember the twins? They're like five years older than us, they graduated before we got to high school. They're her sisters, and her other sister you gotta remember. Her name is Ryan. She was two years ahead of us."

Castle's eyes light up.

"Oh yeah! I remember Ryan. She was kinda crazy. But yeah, I remember her sister. We never spoke or nothing, I used to just see her in traffic."

Lock begins where he left off.

"When I first graduated high school, well, when we graduated high school, I sold a lot of my stuff since I knew I was gonna be leaving after the summer. I don't know if you remember, but I had a few phones for sale too. Chrissy hit me up on FaceBook and said that her sister wanted the phone. So we went back and forth about that for a little while, but then we kinda sparked up a separate conversation too. We inboxed a lot and texted each other too, but I know you remember, I left for school early. I was hardly home that summer. Plus she was kinda back and forth dealing with somebody, so we just left it there. Fast forward to the next summer. I get home from school, and I eventually decide to hit her up. We picked it right back up. So at some point we decide to meet up. Now keep in mind, she still kinda has this dude in the picture, but I guess he wasn't acting right. She came to my spot at like 4 in the morning."

Castle interrupts him there.

"The first time y'all met up?"

Lock responds

"Yeah bro but listen, so I'm being respectful, I didn't even try it. We sit there talking and watching TV. When she goes to leave, I walk her to the door and we start to kiss, I kinda felt the energy, and now looking back on it now, I'm sure it coulda happened that night."

Castle jumps in

"Nigga! What the hell is wrong with you?"

"That's not it" Lock utters.

"So we kept talking, and I liked her. Like for real. But I knew she had that situation lingering in the background. We got together quite a few more times and we never fucked. Of course I'm kicking myself for not fucking her, but I really felt like I should have tried harder to make something out of it. I didn't give it a full push 'cause I was thinking that life was gonna get in the way, you know, I had to leave and she had stuff going on. I was thinking, maybe she's too invested in him to totally drop him for me. Then he found out about us. Not really about me, but he found out that there was a me. She messaged me one day and said 'He doesn't know who you are, but he knows that you exist.' After that, we slowed down. We probably only talked a few times after that. We talked and FaceTimed a few times when I was at school, but the distance between us at that point made it seem far-fetched. Eventually, she ended up getting back with him and getting pregnant. Now they have two kids and so much red tape that I can't get back there. I saw her on FaceBook a few months ago and she looked happy, so I can't even bring myself to try it. I'm guessing I should be happy for her, and I am.... But I'm kinda not. I never told anybody about her. Not a soul. Only one of her friends knew about me."

"Damn nigga, you really kept that secret! If you kept it from me, I know it's real!" Castle says.

"Yeah bro, so that always bugs me how I let that slip through my fingers. Over the last few weeks I gave my life a lot of thought. I weighed a lot of stuff out, and I'm about to make some moves. I'll fill you in as soon as I see how it comes together. I used to watch the movie "Alexander" about Alexander the Great, did you see it?" Lock asks.

Castle replies "I think so."

"There's a line in the movie that says 'Fortune favors the bold' I'm thinking about getting it tatted on my arm. I'm just gonna live like that from now on. All bold moves. We got money to make and dreams to catch," Lock proclaims.

"I'm with you." Castle says.

Then Lock asks "What are you about to do?"

Castle replies "Nothing really."

Lock shakes his hand and says "Word then, I got some things I need to do. I'm gonna stop past Sunoco first and I'll get with you later."

Castle arrives at Reena's house still numbed by Lock's revelation. She answers the door wearing gray sweatpants with two skinny black stripes running down each leg. The top of her sweatpants are rolled over, her form-fitting tee shirt expands to hug her bust as fluidly as it compresses to glide over her lean stomach. It rides up ever so slightly to reveal a pair of Calvin Klein boxers underneath her sweats. Glass of wine in hand, she floats back to the couch in the exact spot she sat before answering the door. She sits with her feet up, one leg vertical and the other resting horizontally. As she tips the goblet to her mouth she asks

"Do you want some?"

Castle responds

"Nah, but if you got some Henny, I'll take it."

She giggles and says

"Now you know I don't."

Then she smacks the cushion next to her and says

"Come sit, let's talk for a minute."

Castle had frozen only a few steps from the door but begins to make his way to the couch. In his mind, the walk across the room plays out like a Hype Williams video. Everything is moving in slow motion except for his brain which is in overdrive. He notices things that he never paid any attention before like how the vent on the wall was secured by six screws and the patina of the floor lamp that seemed to be a factory design. After his hour-long migration to the other side of the room he falls next to her. She angles her body in his direction while Castle remains facing straight ahead, hands resting at his side. Reena reaches over, places her left hand on top of his right as she squeezes gently, she asks,

"Are you alright? Is everything OK?"

She is touching his hand, but he feels it in his stomach. Her hands are soft and warm, tiny compared to his. He notices her perfectly manicured nails painted a shade of nude orange. He sees the tiny remnant of a scar near the knuckle of her pointer finger, evidence of her fall on Star Corner so many years ago. Around her wrist wraps a small rubber bracelet that reads "I Am Trayvon Martin." As he lifts his eyes higher he observes her smile. Her teeth are straight and white. A thin sheet of gloss shimmers over her lips and he imagines that they are as soft as pillows. The siren music of Greek mythology plays softly in his head as he looks into her eyes with such focus that for a second, he marvels in the designs of her irises. Scattering away from her pupil are a thousand bolts of copper lighting. She squeezes his hand a little tighter and says to him,

"I know this is gonna sound crazy, but I'm thinking maybe we should..."

At this moment Castle senses are all exploding. He feels the many paths of the blood flowing through his body and he smells the dull sweetness of Cabernet as it mixes with her perfume in the space between them. He gently grips her hand in response to her clasp upon his. He leans in and then, tap- tap, tap-tap. A knock at the door shatters the monotony, and it is followed by a jiggle of the doorknob. The door opens and Lock comes moseying through. Having what he perceives to be a great day, he's a bit more boisterous than normal.

He yells "What's up?" with a comedic undertone in his voice.

When Reena notices that it is Lock entering, her hand jumps away from Castle's. More of a reflex than a conscious thought. Lock sits in the sofa chair, puts a bag down between his legs and says

" What are y'all talking about?" Before either could answer, he says

"Somebody throw me the remote."

Reena reaches to the table, grabs the remote control and throws it to him. Then she says

"Nothing. What are you up to? How'd your little sit down go?"

"Great!" he replies.

"Castle was there too. We just left not too long ago."

She looks at Castle and says

"Oh, I didn't know you were there too."

By this time, Castle's hopeful euphoria has crashed and burned. He doesn't say anything, only offering a nod.

Lock sits up in his chair and says

"Reena, I wanna talk you about something for a second."

Then he looks over to Castle and says

"You don't mind, right?"

Inside his head, Castle screams

"Hell yeah I mind!"

But only utters the words

"Nah, go ahead."

Lock stands up, and Castle says

"You know what? I'mma just roll out."

Reena says to him

"You can stay."

"Nah, I gotta go." he quickly replies.

Castle doesn't want to leave, but he can't find the heart to stay. He was seconds away from everything that he wanted and fate seemed to snatch it from his fingertips. This walk across the room seems longer than the first and he fractures a little more with each step.

Once alone Lock extends his arm and waves his hand, motioning for Reena to come to him. She ascends from the couch and as she walks closer trying to figure out what's happening, the enigmatic nature of the face she is making gives her the look of puppy dog eyes. Once she reaches him, he grabs her hand while she stands with her wine glass in the other. He says to her

"You love me, right?"

She gives a slight eye roll at the absurdity of the question and responds

"Of course I love you."

Lock then states

"I have a lotta stuff going on right now, my Grand Pop, the music, you know, trying to raise money. I'm reaching out to people, some respond, some don't. I gave a lot of thought to the things I wanna do in life. The places I wanna go, and the level I'm tryna reach."

He pauses for a second and then says,

"I think I work hard enough to get there, I'm really giving it my all."

Reena looks up at him.

"You do work hard. It's gonna happen."

With his eyes pointed at the floor, he smiles and softly says

"Yeah, I know."

As he's lifting his head to look her in the face he says to her

"Through all of that, I came to the conclusion that"

He pauses to take a deep breath.

"I love you, and we should be together."

Chapter 10

NICKELS AND DIMES

At the center of town, a building lay empty, once home to a thriving JC Penney department store. As department stores go, it is a small space, but that never stopped the neighborhood kids from filing in and pretending to look at clothes just so that they could ride the escalator. The entire inside smelled like the pages of the store's famous catalog. Once the corporation closed the location's doors, it was briefly used for storage, but never again opened for retail. It would be that very building where Schemer would attempt his greatest ruse.

Jason Deloatch was the youngest of three kids born into what could easily be described as a chaotic environment. His Dad drank and played video games all day while his mom worked two jobs. His parents fought over everything, and as time went on his father's fuse grew shorter and shorter. By the time Jason was 6 years old, it was well understood that talking back, or even bringing his dad's drink from the refrigerator too slowly could easily result in a slap or even a closed fisted punch. His mother tried her best to bring normalcy to her kids' lives-she bought them more than she could afford and almost never said no. She was a shining light in an otherwise dreary existence, but she worked so many hours that she was hardly ever around. When she was at home she mostly argued with Jason's dad who always became violent, and the cops were often called. Like clockwork, he would be back in a day or two like nothing had ever happened. Jason learned at an early age that he couldn't physically match his father's aggression, and the only way that he would survive is through manipulation. He began to pay close attention to the smallest details and was soon able to predict reactions before they occurred. He began only analyzing his father, but soon began to look for things that he could find in anyone he came across. He didn't understand it at the time, but he was becoming an expert on human behavior patterns and it all began as he was looking for ways to not get slapped in the face or punched in the gut. Self-preservation had taught him more than most people ever get from any psychology degree.

The natural order of things is to progress. As Jason grew older he began to maneuver through situations so that he would emerge as the primary benefactor. He always came out on top. As a scrawny 12-year-old, Jason came to the attention of a kid named Rich. He was in the 8th grade, which was a grade up from Jason, but Rich had also been held back a year. He stood nearly six feet tall, had a full mustache and he wanted Jason's money every day. What was Jason going to do? Telling his teachers or the principal would label him a snitch and life would be hell. Not to mention that after being branded a snitch he would still have to walk home every day. He could stand his ground and fight, but he would most certainly lose, and still have his money ripped from his pockets after being pounded into dust. Jason came up with a plan of which he figured two possible scenarios. The first ended in him ridding himself of the problem. The second scenario ended with him being beaten to a pulp, but since that would be the very same outcome if he didn't pay every day anyway, he felt that it would be wise to at least try.

On his way home from school, he stopped at Hank's and purchased a basketball card price guide. These books give the value a card can be bought or sold for. They list thousands of cards with release dates spanning decades. Jason knew that Rich was a sports fan, and he overheard Rich talking about owning and trading cards a few times before at the lunch table. When Jason returned to school the next day, he told Rich that he could not pay him on that day because it was of utmost importance that he bought the price guide. He went on to tell Rich about the thousands of cards which he owned and how his father had been collecting them since before he was born, and passed the collection on to him. In actuality, there was no extensive collection and the only cards that Jason owned were 131 cards which were all high-quality replicas, but essentially worthless. Each card carries a value of about 20 cents. Their authentic counterparts, however, ranged anywhere from $5 to $500. Jason told Rich that he would go home that night and highlight the cards that he owned and instead of paying Rich every day, he would sell him cards at huge discounts at a rate of one per week. Jason knew that with 52 weeks in a year, he had enough cards to last almost three school years. Rich took the book home and when Jason reached school the next day Rich was waiting for him with excitement in his eyes. He went on and on about how great the cards were that Jason owned, and how he just had to have them. Jason pretended to not care about the cards even though they supposedly held value. He did this to make it seem more believable that he would be willing to part ways with them for such a low price. He also played up a sense of friendship to Rich, stroking his bully ego into believing that it was being done out of some sort of homage. Jason had managed to get his hands on all 131 cards three months prior for less than $15 total and in the first month he'd already made $37 selling four cards to Rich. His plan could not have worked any better. Not only did he find a solution for paying money out of his pocket by turning it around to earn him money, but he also gained a bodyguard of sorts. Rich protected his cash cow at all costs, and anyone who had a problem with Jason had a problem with Rich. By the end of the school year, Jason was $173 richer while only parting ways with 19 cards.

Many people associate the "con" in con artist with convict. Either that or they believe that con is a term which means to swindle. Truth is, it is actually an abbreviation for the word confidence, or confidence man. One day Jason surfed the internet for a report that he was to write on the Boston Tea Party, instead, he typed "get rich quick" into the Google bar and found the story of Charles Ponzi. Jason was completely mesmerized by the way Ponzi at one point had people begging to give him money. He read everything that he could find about Ponzi and the scheme that bore his name. Eventually, he went on to study all of the great con men from Victor Lustig to Soapy Smith. His favorite movie became "Catch Me If You Can" about the life of a famous con artist Frank Abagnale, Jr. Still just a kid, Jason thought there was no way for him to get people to give him millions of dollars so a Ponzi scheme was out of the question, but he would learn all there was to know about how these confident men became rich and applying it where he could. From that point on he focused on not much else. He learned a scam that frequently worked-tricking store clerks into handing over free money. He would try this scam every opportunity he got, and if for some reason the clerk was able to catch on, he would act really confused and claim it to be an honest error of judgement. By this time he was still only 14 but very persuasive, and managed to never have the cops called while running the trick. He would shop at a gas station or convenience store, and he would pay for a small item like a pack of gum. The item was always less than one dollar. He would give the clerk a $10 bill. Jason would get back either nine ones and the change or a five dollar bill plus four one dollar bills and change. Then he would tell the clerk he has an extra one and would like to exchange his ten ones or five dollar bill and five ones for a ten. The most critical part of the scam is when he would reach out his hand in an effort to get the clerk to hand him the ten dollar bill before handing over the one dollar bills. Once he had done that successfully, he would then give the clerk nine ones and the ten dollar bill. The clerk would then almost always assume he made a mistake and offer to exchange the ten that they are at that point holding for a one dollar bill. That is when Jason would say to the clerk "Here, take another one, just give me twenty and call it even." What he did every single time was swap ten dollars for twenty dollars because the ten dollar bill was the store's money. Jason made hundreds of dollars using this simple yet effective technique, while only having it sniffed out a few times.

By the time Jason turned 15, he earned a reputation for finding clever ways to make money. When some of his friends turned to the drug game, Jason stayed away from that, choosing to focus on brainy ways to get paid. His friends began to call him Schemer, an ode to an unreleased Nas track titled "Day Dreamin, Stay Schemin." The running joke was that Jason spent his days dreaming of plots to get rich, he stayed scheming. One day he ran into his aunt's ex-boyfriend Reggie, which was a normal occurrence. Reggie was on crack and always came around looking to sell stuff or make deals. This particular day he had his friend with him. A white guy from out of town who Reggie claimed had $10,000 in counterfeit bills. They were looking for $1,000 dollars worth of money or drugs in exchange for the fake bills. Schemer was instantly skeptical, he wondered if Reggie's friend was actually an undercover cop. Schemer did something people rarely do, he asked to see his ID. After grilling them for a few minutes, he pulled Reggie aside and began to go to work on him. He chastised Reggie for bringing some unknown guy around and told him for that reason, the best he could do is five hundred. He also informed him that it would be in the form of cocaine, no cash. Reggie tried to stick to his guns, but Schemer persisted and they eventually settled on seven hundred and fifty dollars. Schemer didn't have that much money lying around, nor did he sell drugs. He immediately called his friend Raheem who he knew would most likely have whatever he needed. He didn't say much to Raheem over the phone except that it would be beneficial for him to get to him quickly. When Raheem arrived, Schemer spoke with him in private away from Reggie and his friend. He made Raheem an offer of one thousand dollars in counterfeit bills for a quarter ounce of coke. Raheem agreed to make the trade and left to get the drugs.

Schemer let Reggie know that the coke would be back soon, but that he and his friend had to leave because his connect would be coming and he didn't want to be seen. Since they already saw Raheem when he arrived, Schemer acted as if Raheem was just a message carrier. He asked Reggie for half of the money up front as a goodwill gesture being as though the drugs were already on the way. Reggie's initial offer was only to let Schemer hold one thousand dollars worth of the bogus currency, but Schemer, of course, talked him into doubling it. Raheem quickly returned with the seven grams of cocaine. Schemer, as promised, gave him the phony bills. The two men shook hands and Schemer promised to call him later.

After Raheem's departure, Schemer rushed to Rite Aid to grab a bottle of B-12 which is often used on a street level to cut cocaine and maximizes profits. He mixed 3 grams of B-12 with the seven grams of cocaine and bagged it into 80 small bags which sell on the street for ten dollars a piece. When Reggie returned, Schemer gave him the 80 bags wrapped in two small sandwich bags. He said to Reggie,

"Five extra in there. You owe me a favor."

He now had nine thousand dollars in counterfeit money, and he hadn't spent a dime of his own money to secure it, other than the nine dollar bottle of B-12. Charles Ponzi would have been proud!

With so much fake money, there's only so many dice games that Schemer could taint before getting his head blown off, so he decided to take it on the road. He still wasn't old enough to drive, which never stopped him before, but he didn't want to take a trip outside of New Jersey with so much on the line while driving without a license. He recruited his older brother Meir and presented him with a plan. They would rent a car from a smoker for the day. Leave early in the morning and hit as many stores as they could. He knew it wouldn't be easy, and that one false move would jam them up, so they meticulously planned a series of disguises so as not to be recognized. One such cloak saw Schemer don a small afro wig underneath a snapback Dodgers hat which when combined looked remarkably natural. To avoid leaving behind fingerprints, they painted fresh coats of clear fingernail polish on their fingertips before entering each store. Meir and Schemer drove from Salem to Prince George County, Maryland before then pivoting, and stopping at every store they found on the journey back home. They made it back to Salem just before midnight and secured just over eight hundred dollars in one day. Frank Abagnale Jr. would have been proud!

***

Upon learning of the party that Lock is throwing in a few days, Schemer calls Attica to suggest that they make a surprise appearance. After all, they had heard nothing from Castle in well over a week. After agreeing to meet with Attica later on, he heads to a meeting which could result in his greatest achievement yet as a man of confidence. He has been working on this ploy for over a month. While traveling into town one day, he noticed a sign that read "We buy houses" followed by a phone number. Schemer called the number and promptly set up a meeting for the man on the other end of the phone to come to view a property that he was looking to sell. Schemer had no such property-instead, he scouted a few abandoned houses in the area and paid for a fake deed to the property. He has an associate who lives in the projects and forges documents, usually pay stubs and rental agreement leases. It cost him only twenty dollars. Next, he had the abandoned house broken into which cost him another ten. He then changed the lock on the front door. This would allow him to act as if the house was rightfully his when it came time for the meeting.

The day before the meeting he began to second guess himself. He thought it would be easily discovered that a barely adult black guy owned a property by himself. He would show up to the meeting and present himself as the true owner's interning assistant. This would buy him time to implant a fake owner who could in turn help pull off the gimmick. He met with the man with whom he had spoken to on the phone, his name was Steven Knight. He introduced himself as Jason, the assistant tasked with walking him through the property. He apologized as his boss had been called away on business at the last minute. Schemer is a chameleon. He uses slang and speaks broken English during leisure conversations, but he can also speak properly with a mastery of the language that would see him accepted on any Ivy League campus. After Mr. Knight has toured the property, he informs him of another property that he wishes for him to see. He then has Mr. Knight follow him to the empty building that was once a JC Penney store on Broadway. He informed Mr. Knight that his boss owned this property as well, and would be letting it go for well under market value in an attempt to settle a separate tax issue. Schemer went on to say that his boss would be back in town in a week and upon his arrival, he would like to meet again to discuss it further. Mr. Knight obliged. Schemer knew that he sparked his interest with the subtle hint that there was quick cash to be made. No scam ever works without a mark who is looking to get something for nothing. Now Schemer was under the gun to produce not only a boss, but a stratagem that Mr. Knight would bite on hook, line and sinker.

Schemer wanted to use a white man as his boss, figuring that it would go over better. Mr. Knight was far less inclined to question the validity of another white male even over the most well-spoken black man.

Schemer reached out to a guy he had done quite a bit of business with from Middletown, Delaware. A computer guy who sold all types of stolen electronics and pirated software. He spent the next few days rehearsing with him what to say and what not to say, as well as completely making up a backstory about inheriting buildings from his dead father. He also spent an entire day having paperwork forged that would lead one to believe that the property could be bought. As scheduled, he met with Mr. Knight, this time introducing him to his boss, Mr. Rubenstein. Schemer knew that faint play ups of stereotypes work wonders, so he created a Jewish boss as the supposed owner of the building. He even had his associate Joe show up wearing a yarmulke. They quickly got to business and explained to Mr. Knight that the building was easily worth one hundred thousand, but the current market sits it in the area of seventy. Joe explained to Mr. Knight that he had a separate tax issue with a property on the other side of town, and his profit in the selling of the JC Penney building would be eaten to satisfy that debt. Rather than go through the normal channels, he would be willing to sell the building for cash at a steep discount. This would allow the transaction to stay off of the books, and would also leave Mr. Knight room to make a quick ten or twenty thousand. To keep Mr. Knight on his heels, Schemer would be sure to politely interrupt, reminding his boss that he had three more meetings about this building today, and to be mindful of time. Another tactic that Schemer used was to bombard Mr. Knight with paperwork. For almost every point that his boss brought up, there was a document to support it, and it would be handed over to Mr. Knight for viewing. Schemer knew that he would not read every document-it was done merely to build Mr. Knight's confidence.

Finally, Joe set a number; he asked for sixty thousand dollars. This was a number far higher than they expected, but they had to leave room to negotiate. Mr. Knight said that he couldn't come up with that much money in cash, using that fact as a way to bargain down. Schemer, again, interrupts and proposes a scenario that he claimed to have spoken to his boss about previously. An instance in which the building and the house that Mr. Knight viewed could be bundled together. For that, his boss would accept twenty thousand dollars up front with the rest of the details being ironed out later. The cost of the house would only add an additional ten thousand on top, but a decision must be made quickly. This is a classic con approach. The mark is given an offer which seems too good to be true with not much time to think about it. Mr. Knight agrees to meet with Joe the next day at which time he will present a cashier's check for twenty thousand dollars. Schemer, in turn, promises both men that he will have all of the necessary paperwork and the keys to both properties ready to hand over. With all of the smoke and mirrors being applied, Mr. Knight never questioned the fact that he had not been inside the vacant store at all. The next day the three men gathered at the vacant house to close the deal. This was strategic-in the event Mr. Knight attempted to use his key it would work, which was not the case at the commercial property. The exchanges were made, and another gathering was scheduled for the following week. Setting their next conference a week out would give Schemer time to cover his tracks before Mr. Knight found out that he had been stiffed. He immediately had the check cashed. He knew cashing it himself would lead directly back to him, so he used Joe to hire a crack addict from Philly. The man was paid $500 and never saw Schemer's face. After the check fees gobbled another $500, Schemer walked away with nineteen thousand dollars. After paying Joe five thousand, Schemer's end tally was fourteen thousand dollars for a scam that cost him in the neighborhood of $400 to finance, most of that being spent on the two prepaid phones used to contact each other and Mr. Knight. Like a bird flying high in the sky, Schemer goes to see Attica. Victor Lustig would be proud!

Schemer arrives at News' apartment still under the influence, high from the rush associated with having money handed over to him in large sums. He is eager to tell of his exploits, and he also tosses Attica a brown paper bag containing fifty crisp $20 bills. So new, that as Attica attempts to count them, some stick together. The unmistakable smell of new money fresh from a bank teller's drawer is intoxicating to

Attica. A totally different fragrance than the wads of crumpled up bills he had grown accustomed to receiving on the block, vastly different yet equally accepted. Schemer asks Attica,

"Is News here?"

"Nah, he left with some jawn about a hour ago," Attica replied.

"Oh, 'cause I wanted to let y'all niggas know what I found out. I'll just tell you though."

"What's up? Start talking then," Attica replies.

Schemer scoots in a little closer to Attica.

"Looks like Castle and his boy Lock got a party coming up this weekend. A couple of rappers with record deals, and a few models are gonna be there. You already know what I'm thinking."

"What's that?" Attica asks.

"Nigga, you already know! We should just pop up. Put them under pressure. Show them that whatever they do, we'll be right there."

Attica slowly nods as if he agrees.

"I'm with that." he says.

Schemer snaps his fingers three times in rapid succession and says,

"Oh! I almost forgot! They're trying to sign this boy from Salem named Damani. You probably don't know him, he's a little younger than me. His rap name is Stylez. He had a song that was buzzing a few months back."

Attica jumps in and says

"Man, I don't give a fuck about these corny ass new rappers that can't fucking rap. I probably didn't hear that shit."

Schemer replies

"Yeah, I feel you, but that ain't the point I was making. They're trying to sign him and this guy is out here running his mouth about how he's about to blow up, and how much money is coming. He's pillow talking to this jawn named Niya and she be telling me everything. This bitch can't hold water. We can keep the pressure on them from the front, and keep getting info outta this bitch in the back. Before you know it we can have everything. Lock and Castle will just be working for us."

Attica gives a short laugh and says,

"Alright then. Saturday. Let's show up."

Schemer asks,

"You think News is gonna roll?"

Attica twists his lip and replies,

"You know that nigga don't like going to parties. I'll see if I can talk him into it though."

Schemers adds,

"Yeah, but I think it will play out better if he shows up. Just his presence will scare the shit out of them."

Both men share a quick laugh. Then Schemer remembers the other story he wanted to tell.

"You ain't gonna believe this bro. So I sold a building today...."

Chapter 11

YOU WON'T SEE ME TONIGHT

Salem is one of the oldest cities in the northeast. Older than Philadelphia, a treasure chest of history echoes through the South Jersey town. Over the years, much of that history has been subtly preserved through monuments and honorary namings. There's Gibbon Street, named for the wealthy family which carried the surname, most notably Quinton Gibbon, a very successful medical doctor. Then there is Sinnickson Street, immortalizing Clement Hall Sinnickson who was born and died in Salem and served in the United States House of Representatives. A small park, more like a plot of grass behind the county superior courthouse and just on the other side of the parking lot, stands dedicated to a member of the Layton family, wealthy business owners and politicians who planted roots in Salem years ago. There is even a park with a small half-domed stage named for MLK where bands play free concerts during the summer months. Noticeably (or maybe not so noticeably) absent is perhaps the greatest and most accomplished child of the city born of African descent.

John S. Rock made his way into the world in October of 1825. He was formally educated to completion, which was not the common practice of the day, especially for Blacks. For four years he worked as a teacher in a one-roomed school in Salem, but ambition is a fire which unsettles. While teaching, Rock also apprenticed under two white doctors and eventually applied for medical school. He was denied based on his race which led him to pursue dentistry. After gaining notoriety as a masterful dentist, he was finally granted entry into medical school and graduated from The American Medical College in Philadelphia, becoming one of the first Black doctors in the entire country. By the age of 27, John Rock had established himself as an accomplished teacher, dentist and doctor. He would also become a noted abolitionist, sharing the stage on several occasions with Frederick Douglass, and it was during this period that Rock is credited with coining the popular phrase "Black Is Beautiful." Rock would fall ill, causing him to seek medical attention outside of the country. His doctors urged him to cut his workload, which prompted Rock to give up his medical practices. Rock then began to study law. He would go on to pass the Massachusetts Bar, and opened a private practice there in Boston. He then went on to become the first African American attorney admitted to the Bar of the Supreme Court of the United States, and the first Black ever to be received on the floor of the House of Representatives. Not a single street, park or even plaque exists inside the city in his remembrance, nor is he mentioned in the section of the school system's curriculum which covers local history.

As a freshman in college, Lock attended a lecture entitled "Famous Firsts in Black America". These events were free for students to attend, and Lock was so excited to be out on his own and away from home that he found himself attending functions of this sort just because he could. Lock scribbled into his notebook as the topic twisted and turned through years of accomplishments. He began drawing a circle, and giving it a ring like the planet Saturn after the name Jupiter Hammon was introduced. Saturn and Jupiter are two totally separate planets, but for some reason he drew Saturn anyway. Jupiter Hammon was the first known Black author to be published. Lock heard about Alexander Twilight becoming the first Black man to receive a degree from an American college. Normally, one in constant search of historical facts, Lock just wasn't feeling it that day. He was seconds away from getting up to leave when John Stewart Rock's name was mentioned. This meant nothing more to Lock that the countless others who had been discussed up to that point. Everything changed when the lecturer stated with no special emphasis that Rock had been born in Salem, NJ. Lock's antennas shot up into full transmission. He was pulled back in with a laser focus.

After leaving the event he immediately called Reena to see if she had ever heard of John Rock. He wondered how he managed to make it to adulthood, having lived in Salem every day of his life, and not once hearing his name. Reena was a straight-A student ever since they started getting grades. She once cried for a week because there was a possibility that she would get a B. Lock felt that if anyone had heard of him, it would be Reena. He called her but she didn't pick up; however, she called him back.

"Hello."

"Hey boy, what are you doing?" she asked.

Lock responds "I'm good. Yo, have you ever heard of a dude named John Rock?"

"Rockefeller?" she asked.

Lock sighed and with conviction said,

"I know who Rockefeller is, this guy was named Rock. John S. Rock."

Reena thought for a second and finally responded,

"Uh, no, I don't think I do. Why?"

With excitement now in his voice he begins to explain.

" I was at this lecture, and they were going over Black people who were the first to do all of this different stuff. So I'm sitting there listening, but for some reason I was getting bored, and I kinda zoned out for a second. So he's going on and on, and he starts talking about this guy named John S. Rock, but then he said that he was born in Salem. Can you believe that? He was the first Black man on the floor of the House of Representatives, and he started the saying "Black Is Beautiful! That's crazy, right!?"

"Really?" Reena replied. "I wonder why we never heard about him."

"I was thinking the same thing." Lock said to her.

Reena then stated

"I'm gonna look him up as soon as we get off of the phone."

When she did her research, it was all there. She and Lock spoke about John S. Rock a bunch of times over those next few weeks, proud that such an important person in history was born in Salem. Lock said to Reena during one of their talks, "They taught us about John Fenwick and the Indians every damn year, but never told us this. I don't understand how."

Reena agreed, and they promised to do something about it. That conspiracy would sit un-acted upon for a few years until after Lock graduated college and returned to Salem. It was then that they decided to petition the city. They asked that a street be renamed after a great man who once upon a time called Salem his home. The politics of the matter has taken time and they have yet to receive an answer from the city, but both Lock and Reena are resolute in seeing it through.

***

Event days are always stressful for Lock. No matter how well things are planned, something is bound to go wrong. Philly rappers can be some of the biggest divas out there, and he has two lined up for the party. Multiply that by the models who are also set to attend and that equals a multitude of phone calls to management teams that Lock must make and receive, which usually reach a near deafening crescendo about an hour or so after an event kicks off. Today is no different. The DJ is late, he hasn't heard from either artist and his phone battery is down to 17 percent. In the midst of hurry and confusion he left his charger on the living room table. He stands in the empty DJ booth overlooking the hushed venue thinking to himself "What have I done for God to hate me so much?". After wallowing in pity for about 45 seconds he snaps himself out of it. This is nothing new and things always work out. He heads to the bathroom to make sure that his outfit is still as great as it was when he left the house. He gazes at himself in the mirror for a second, the blue lenses of his Porsche Design sunglasses almost perfectly accent his Assuré Arman shirt spelling out "Broke" across the chest. His distressed Balmain jeans taper just enough at the ankle that they don't hang over his Sean Wotherspoon Air Max 97's. One last check of his haircut and his confidence has returned as he heads back to the area of the future dance floor. Castle arrives minutes after the DJ and the two go over everything one last time while the DJ sets up his equipment.

The first couple of hours are pure uneasy energy for a promoter. Most people don't show up to parties early, so the man whose money and reputation are on the line is a nervous wreck in those moments. Lock hides it well as he exudes nothing but confidence, while inside his chest is fluttering with butterflies and his stomach is unsettled mess. No amount of planning and advertising can guarantee a solid turnout, but as more people begin to file in, Lock feels increasingly more jovial. Stylez finally appears and is more than impressed by not only the turnout, but also by the type of people in attendance. It is far more than he is used to, and only reaches new heights as Lock shuffles him into the VIP section. Though the models have yet to land, there is no shortage of women far beyond suitable as far as appearance goes. Stylez sees Castle and approaches the booth to greet him. He is a tiny bit preoccupied adding to his Snapchat story, flashing a bottle of D Ussé while allowing one of the girls to sport his chain in the video. After grandstanding for the camera, Castle waves his arm signaling for Stylez to come over. The music is blaring so to hear clearly they have to talk directly into one another's ear.

"Yo, you good?" Castle asks.
Without a thought Stylez responds
   "Yeah bro, I'm straight! It's lit in here. I'm trying to see what I can get."
Castle laughs.
   "You can definitely leave with something. It'll be way more in here a little later. You ready to perform though?"
Stylez ensures Castle
   "Hell yeah! I can't wait to burn this bitch down."
Castle reaches for a handshake and says
   "Say no more. I can't wait to see you do your thing bro."

The models file into the club and directly to the VIP section, which sways a large portion of the crowd in that direction like a tidal wave. Extra bottles are hurried over and onlookers snap pictures and videos feverishly. One of the models, wearing a hot pink body-hugging dress, leans over the railing to participate in a few of the many over the shoulder selfies she has been asked to participate in. A current floods through the entire building, an underlying sense of participation in something epic. Some nights the perfect DJ plays the perfect records with the perfect mix of people in attendance and mere words fail miserably at posterity. The ultimate "You had to be there" moment, and it never happens again until it happens again. The smell that spilled alcohol makes infused with the moist vapor of smoke machines is a unique fragrance that defines the blue streaking 20's of habitual partygoers. For three minutes at a time nothing else in the world matters as the bass pours out of the speakers and penetrates every soul in reach of its quake. Lock thrives inside this contained chaos and rarely feels more alive.

Reena rolls into the club accompanied by Milan and Monae. They would have made it much earlier, but each of the three changed clothes a minimum of three times. Reena is wearing hip huggers with thigh length, high heel boots which are of a deep burgundy shade. Her loose armed button-down shirt is knotted at the waist with a plunging neckline. Her baby hair is perfectly placed and her six straight back cornrows are twisted into a bun behind her head. A pair of gold-framed aviator glasses with clear lenses shimmer as she strides through the floor with the conviction of a drum major. Monae follows crowned in a mane of natural curls. The smokey eyeshadow thrusts forward the brightness of her eyes and they shine like crushed glass bathing in sunlight. Her olive green dress looks tailor-made to fit with its choker style collar above a square cleavage cutout. Her hips run away from her slender waist and her legs are solid tree trunks yet equally sleek. Milan brings up the rear, her honey blonde silk press is just past shoulder length. Her hazel eyes are an enigmatic mixture of inviting and standoffish. The overly full lips that got her teased as a kid are now a welcomed attribute drawing attention and envy-glossed to perfection, as if she is seconds removed from tongue kissing a glass of water. Her black Mi'Aash Manière split waist catsuit boasts aerodynamics that Italian automakers would kill for, only broken by the thin jacket distressed nearly to shreds that flanks her from the ribs up. Her 6-inch red bottom heels force her hips to sway back and forth like a pocket watch dangling from the hand of a skilled hypnotist. Her pendulum-esque motion affords an equal effect as it entrances nearly everyone whose eyes have been helplessly drawn to her. They garner nearly as many stares as the models did as they make their way directly to VIP.

Lock has been seldom seen as he darts around ensuring that the event flows smoothly while Castle has made the VIP his oyster, giving his attention to girl after girl, undivided however brief. He asks one of his newly found acquaintances to take a picture of him. He exits the booth and makes his way to the railing and stands for an over the back shot of him seemingly surveying the crowd. As he poses for the still frame he noticed that the crowd is bouncing up and down, yet there is a dead spot moving slowly in his direction. Creeping forward calmly and steadily with zero bounce. As he focused and then focuses even harder he realizes that the huddled mass floating nearer like the blob is just as scary; Bad News, Schemer and Attica. He stands there motionless, as stoic as Honest Abe, all jubilation having been washed from his face like loose sands during a flash flood. As the three men approach the security standing guard at the VIP entrance Attica points at Castle after being denied entrance. The guard turns and looks at Castle who reluctantly motions for the three men to be granted access. As they enter and file by, Attica smacks Castle on the shoulder and says to him

"Let me talk to you for a minute."

Castle follows them to a third booth next to the section occupied by Reena, Milan and Monae. Castle sits last and Attica asks
"So what's going on? Thought you skipped town or something."

"Nah, I'm around." Castle replies.
"So, I take it that you ain't got my money yet, so I just came to see how our party was going."

Castle sits like a chastised child, fighting back the urge to lash out, knowing that a swift harsh punishment would be imminent.
"Well you know I don't have a quarter mill, so what can I do?" Castle asks.

"Nigga, the clock is ticking, and it ain't too many ticks left." Attica screams in an attempt to be heard over the music. Then he says to Castle
"I'll just be looking for my cut out of tonight's profits then." as he shrugs his shoulders.
"That's not my call." Castle pleads.

"Well make it your call muthafucka! I'm tired of waiting, and you think it's a fucking game out here!" Attica yells.

Castle gets up from the booth and leans back down to be heard as he says
"I'm gonna try my best."

He heads directly to find Lock. After a few minutes, he finally catches up to him in the kitchen where Lock had gone to escape the music as he talked on the phone.
"Yo man, I need to talk to you," Castle says with urgency.
Lock pulls the phone from his ear and places it against his chest as if to block the person on the other end from hearing him say
"One second bro, let me clear this up real quick, hold on."
He then places the phone back to his ear and continues where he left off.
"Listen, I already have the opening act here ready to go, but I'm not putting him on stage until your guy is here. I can't get the crowd ready and risk them having to wait if your guy is late."
He listens for a second and then pulls the phone from his ear again. In a soft, almost whispery voice he asks Castle
"Can you check on the raffle? See how much we made so far. If it's not at least five hundred, switch out the girl with that big titty jawn up front at the door. Tell her to apply the pressure."
He again put the phone back to his ear with his left hand while also reaching out with his right hand to give Castle a fist bump. He mouths the words "Thank you, bro" before again addressing the person on the phone.
"That's fine, just remember that the price goes down for every minute that he's late."

Reena, Milan and Monae have just made it back into VIP after heading to the dance floor for a few songs. As they file into the booth, Schemer takes note and urges News and Attica to follow him on his quest to try his luck.
He leans in and says
"It's three of them and three of us, let's make it happen."

Attica twists his lip, tilts his head and says
"Fuck it, let's go."

News doesn't say a word, he just follows suit.
"Ladies, do you mind if we sit with y'all?" Attica asks.

Reena never looks up from her phone to acknowledge the question and before Milan could open her mouth, Monae says,
"Sure, have a seat."

Milan gives her the death stare. She was going to tell them that the seats were taken. The three men sit down and pleasantries are exchanged. Monae, being so genuinely kind-hearted and courteous, often carries on conversation with men who approach her, which causes them to confuse her graciousness for mutual attraction. Milan on the other hand has shoulders that can grow as cold as a windy February night. Reena has mastered the art of the cute smile followed by a line that is always somewhere in the area of "Aww, that's so nice, but I can't." The three women are playing their natural roles to perfection as Monae and Schemer converse so fluidly that he honestly believes that his chances are much higher than they actually are. Milan is wearing her best Maleficent face while attempting to channel the soul of Eva Dandridge as Attica asks her the normal icebreaker questions. She thinks to herself,
"He's cute, but no way."
Reena is being just nice enough to not be labeled a bitch, but distant enough to send the message that she is not interested. News continues on with his efforts, and finally asks her,
"You got a boyfriend or something?"
Reena replies, "Not really."
Then, shooting her eyes at the ceiling, she takes a deep breath and says,
"I have a lot going on though."

Attica orders three bottles of Rosé in an attempt to lower the group's guard. He thinks maybe the sound of corks popping and drinks flowing will jumpstart the conversation. Milan's apathy has the reverse effect on Attica; only serves to enhance his willingness to chase. Milan's phone rings, and she answers it using the pointer finger of her opposite hand to plug her ear. She yells into the phone
"OK, I'll be up there in a second."
She hangs up the phone and says to everyone at the table
"I'll be right back."

Reena asks
"Where are you going?"

Milan quickly replies,

"Nowhere girl, I'm coming right back."

As Milan heads out of the VIP section Attica asks Monae
"What's up with your girl?"

Monae flips her hand and says,
"Oh nothing. She's cool, it just takes her a while to open up."

Milan reaches the entrance and is greeted by a tall, busty, golden-skinned female.
Milan informs the woman at the booth that her friend, Ariel Carl, is on the list and can
enter without paying admission. She then advises the woman to give Ariel the bracelet
needed to buy drinks and the one necessary to enter VIP. They enter the walkway
between the lobby and the floor of the club where Milan says to Ariel
"He's wearing a blue shirt that says 'Broke' on the front and some Porsche glasses.
You already know what to do, but text me if you need to."

Ariel responds,
"Yeah girl, I got you."

They enter the dance floor and part ways. Milan heads back to her crew and Ariel
searches for Lock. She finds him by the DJ booth having a conversation with a
refrigerator moonlighting as a security guard. They are laughing with one another
which leads Ariel to believe that it is not a business conversation, therefore she feels
free to approach.

"Hey handsome. How are you?"

Stunned, Lock replies,
"I'm good, how about you?"

Ariel brushes his hand ever so gently with the back of her own hand and says,
"I'm fine, what's your name?"

Trying with every fiber in his body not to look at her cleavage he replies
"You can call me Lock. How about you? What's your name?"

"Lock like a door?" she asks.
"Hi Lock like a door, I'm Ariel." and extends her hand.

Lock obliges, and as they partake in the most basic of greeting traditions Lock ask her
"So what part of Philly are you from?"

"Southwest" she replies.

"Born and raised?" he asks.

"Yeah, why?" she asks with lighthearted inquisitiveness.

Lock fails to hold back laughter as he asks
"On the playground is where you spent most of your days?"

It takes Ariel a quick second to get it, but then she playfully slaps him on the arm and says
"No stupid, I said Southwest not West."
Ariel wraps her pinky around Lock's pointer finger and says to him
"Let me buy you a drink."

Lock replies
"Nah, I'm good, but thanks though. I don't really drink like that. Maybe once or twice a year."

Ariel sticks out her bottom lip like a pouting child and says,
"Come on, just one. For me?"

Her pout then transforms into a magazine worthy smile. As she begins to turn and walk in the direction of the bar still holding Lock by the finger, he catches a brief glimpse of her eyes with cascading lashes and perfectly placed liner swooping out so beautifully that Amy Winehouse would be green with envy. As if the pied piper had sparked a tune, Lock was no longer in control and found himself walking toward the bar without ever making a conscious decision to take a step. Once there, he orders a shot of 1942 while Ariel opts for Hennessy.

"1942 Flows, huh?" she asks.

Lock replies

"Yeah, I used to pray for times like this."

He laughs a little at his corny Meek Mill reference, then he tells her,

"I don't drink a lot, so I never got to a chance check it out after the song came out. So here's my chance I guess."

He is trying to figure out where this is coming from because even the most attractive guys don't get hit on as much as a slightly below average woman, and here is a girl among the prettiest in the building nearly throwing herself at him. "Must be my lucky day!" he thinks to himself. Lock's phone is sitting on the bar and Ariel picks it up. She turns it around to face Lock and says

"Unlock it for me."

Lock apprehensively types in his four digit code then as she begins to tap on the screen he steps around to view from over her shoulder what she is doing. She texts "Hey sexy!" followed by a winking emoji to herself from Lock's phone. Then she saves her number in his phone with a heart-eyed and then a splash emoji following her name. They continue talking for the next half hour, which in club time translates to about three weeks.

While still conversing with Ariel, a bottle girl approaches Lock and informs him that a group in VIP has refused to pay a large bill. She was told by someone in the group that it should be on the house and to talk to the promoter. Lock excuses himself and goes to make sense of the situation. The bottle girl points him in the right direction and once he arrives, he sees the three men sitting with Reena, Milan and Monae. Lock recognizes News immediately, and he is almost sure of Attica's identity. It's been over 7 years since the last time he had seen Attica, and they never spoke nor have they ever been close. Attica is older than Lock and stayed in the streets, Lock rarely hung out in those areas. In a very pleasant voice Lock asks the table collectively

"Is everything OK here?"

He avoids any eye contact with Reena, choosing to focus on the men at the table. Schemer replies,

"Yeah man, we're good over here. You need something?"

Lock squeezes his hands together.

"Yes, I was told that there was a misunderstanding about bottles that were purchased. Those aren't free. Someone here is responsible for that bill."

Attica waves his finger from side to side and says

"You better get your boy Castle over here. He'll straighten it out."

Lock then turns and peers into the crowd. He motions to a member of security to tap Castle on the shoulder as he stands at the bar. The security guard does just that and after gaining Castle's attention, he points up to the VIP section where Lock is standing. With a swift hard jerk of the arm, Lock emphatically demands Castle's presence. Castle approaches the table and asks,

"What's going on?"
There's a lump in Castle's throat, and his thoughts are running in six different directions. He wanted to tell Lock everything before it came to this. Feeling backed into a corner, he asks,
"Attica, can we talk over here for a minute?"

Castle then places his palm over Lock's shoulder blade and guides him away from the table and into a section where the three can speak privately. They gather in a circle, and Castle addresses the situation.
"Look, I'll take care of the bottles." he says to Lock.

Turning his attention to Attica, he states
"But no more. I can't afford to keep paying for that shit."

Attica smirks and replies
"That's not my problem."

No sooner than his words touch the air, Lock aggressively states
"Man, fuck that shit. I'm not paying for these fucking bottles and neither are you!"

Attica, in a misdirection form of conversation, looks Castle squarely in the eyes but speaks words meant to reach Lock.
"It doesn't matter, it's all our money anyway."

Absolutely puzzled, Lock says
"What?"

"Oh, he doesn't know?" Attica replies comedically.

"I'll tell you what I do know" Lock states. "I know who you are but I don't know you like that and you don't know me, so ain't no 'our' nothing!"

Like a feisty Chihuahua nipping at the foot of a Rottweiler, Attica felt about as threatened by Lock's fiery decree as a stroll through Mr. Rogers' Neighborhood. He walks away, essentially exiting the conversation, but not before saying,
"I'll let y'all talk. Castle don't forget about my cut."

Lock instantly turns to Castle with brimstone in his eyes.
"What the hell is he talking about?" he asks.

With a pitiful look Castle states "Look bro, we gotta talk. Let's go back to the kitchen real quick."

Seconds after Attica returns to the booth Lock and Castle storm by. Reena is so busy feigning that she doesn't see the men parade by. Milan astutely recognizes not only the body language of the two best friends, but the looks on their faces as well. She gets up from her seat and says,
"I'll be right back."

Attica says to her
"Damn, again?"

Milan totally disregards the statement and hurries away on the same path Lock and Castle blazed through only moments before. When Lock and Castle file into the kitchen, Lock spins into a 180 and screams,
"Tell me something bro, what the fuck is this dude talking about?!"

Castle begins to stutter, but eventually manages in a crackling voice, almost as if he is holding back tears to say,
"Remember when we put the bread up to get stuff started? Well I got some of it from him. I tried to pay him back but he got locked up and now it's outta control and I don't know what to do bro, I'm sorry."

Lock grabs two fistfuls of Castle's shirt, snatched him closer and screams,
"What the fuck do you mean you're sorry!? This shit can't happen!"

Milan stood outside the door for just about the entire conversation waiting for the perfect opportunity to swoop in and plant her seed of uncertainty. She barges through the door and proclaims
"You two been friends way too long to be fighting over Reena! Stop it!"

Without ever letting go of Castle's shirt, Lock asks Milan
"What? Why would we be fighting over her?"

Milan gasps and covers her mouth with her hand and then says
"Oh, she didn't tell you? My bad."

Milan turns to walk away and Lock asks her,
"Tell me what?"

"It's not my place to say. I'm sorry." she replies as she exits the room.

Milan and Reena got dressed together earlier when preparing for the party. They've done so hundreds of times and it's always the same, a sink full of curling irons, eyeshadow, lipstick and edge control, clothes and shoes flung all over the bed and floor while music plays in the background. These moments also act as impromptu therapy sessions and they cover any relative issue. In the latest installment, Reena spilled her heart out to Milan about developing confusing feelings for Castle and being so quickly taken aback by Lock's confession. Wanting Lock for herself, Milan gave Reena the most ambiguous advice that she could drum up which only helped to confuse Reena even more. Milan on the other hand gained valuable information to use in her quest to drive a wedge between the two star-crossed almost lovers.

Lock storms back into the dance area and up the steps into the VIP. He asks Reena
"Can I speak to you for a second?"

Reena sees the urgency in his eyes and quickly rises to her feet. She exits the booth and then huddles in a corner just a little further down from where Lock just finished wrapping up his fateful exchange with Attica and Castle. He asks Reena,
"Is something going on with you and Castle?"

Startled by the last thing she expected to hear Reena replies,
"What? What makes you ask that?"

Undeterred by Reena's off-balanced deflection, he says to her
"Don't worry about it, answer the question."

"No! Why?" she pleads.

"Aight" he says, and then turns to walk away but with two hands Reena grabs him
by the arm right above where his elbow bends. She states
"Let's talk later. I wanted to talk to you anyway and we never..... Well let's just talk
later. You wanna meet up after here? Meet me at the diner."

"Yeah, that's cool." he says.

"Which one?" Reena asks.

"Either Woodbury or Deepwater. I guess let's just hit Woodbury since it's closer."
Lock says.

Finally letting his arm go Reena says,
"OK, I'll see you there."

Lock hustles out of the VIP and disappears into the crowd. The massive circus that
has just ensued has caused him to neglect his responsibilities for a huge gap of time.
Confused and frustrated he eventually finds himself back at the bar looking to have
another drink. He orders a shot of Henny and no sooner than the bartender skips away
to pour his drink, he feels fingers gently slide across the back of his neck. It sends
chills shooting down his spine which, without a thought, causes him to shrug his
shoulders. He makes an about-face to find Ariel smiling like the Cheshire.
"I was looking for you." she says. "I thought you were hiding from me."

"Nah, a lot just popped off and I had to run around. Look, the show is about to
start. Do you wanna go on the stage with me?" Lock asks.

"Of course." she replies. He takes her by the hand and gently whips her out in
front of them as they head to the stage.

The performances were all amazing and high energy. Lock is supremely impressed
with Stylez, though his mind still partially remains in the kitchen, trying to breakdown
and decipher the two major bombshells Hiroshima and Nagasaki that were dropped on

him less than a minute apart. Lock goes through the motions but is completely preoccupied. Still probing, Ariel asks Lock,

"So, I never asked, are you single?"

Lock sighs, then replies,

"Do you want the long answer or the short answer?"

Before Ariel can say a word he says to her,

"Nah, the long answer is way too much. Basically, I don't know how to answer that."

"So I'll take that as a no. You don't have a girlfriend." she purrs somewhat seductively.

"Sounds cliché, but it's complicated." Lock replies.

As the night draws to a close Lock notices that Castle has disappeared. The lights turn on, which is the official sign that the festivities have commenced and Lock surveys wall to wall looking for Castle. As Reena makes her way to the door behind Monae and ahead of Milan, she and Lock make eye contact and both nod yes to each other. In some telepathic way, that means that they still agree to meet at the diner and it is mutually understood. Just as they are about to exit Milan tugs on Reena's arm and says,

"Y'all go ahead. Remember the boy, Chris, that I used to talk to? He's here and I'm gonna ride home with him."

Reena, not feeling comfortable leaving Milan alone asks,

"Are you sure?"

"Yeah girl, I'm fine. I'll text you when I get home." Milan assures.

"OK, I'll talk to you soon." Reena says before turning and exiting.

Milan heads back into the club against the flow of traffic spilling out. She sees Lock over by the bar surrounded by members of the security team. She walks over, gives Lock a hug and congratulates him on a successful event.

"What are you drinking? One last shot on me to celebrate." she says to him.

"D'Usse" he replies.

On the other side of the bar sits Ariel, typing into her phone, patiently waiting for Lock to finish. Lock is so transfixed with finishing the last bit of business so that he can leave that he doesn't notice that Ariel is still at the bar. Milan gets the bartender's attention who is done serving and now cleaning. Last call expired long ago, but Milan tells her that the drinks are for Lock so she pours them. With Lock still winding down his conversation and paying the security team it was a cinch for her to crack open a clear small capsule of Molly and dump it into his drink. She stays at the bar for a second pretending to send a text, but in actuality she is waiting for the cloudiness in his shot to dissolve. She walks over with a shot in each hand, careful to hand Lock the correct glass.

"Cheers!" she says, and they knock back their respective drinks simultaneously.

"What are you doing when you leave here?" Milan asks.

Lock tells her,
"I'm meeting Reena at the diner. We gotta talk about some stuff."

"Oh, OK." Milan says. "Well I'm gonna wait for you. Can you walk me out?"

"Yeah, no doubt, just give me a minute to finish up in the back and I'll be right back" Lock replies.

He vanishes into a back room. Milan sits at the bar talking to Ariel, quietly going over the latter half of the plan. Several minutes later, Lock emerges from the room on rubbery legs. Milan hops up and grabs his arm to steady him. The moment her hand touches him the sensation of being tickled by a thousand feathers begins spread over his entire body.

"The floor is moving?" he says to Milan.

"Walk over here and sit down, come on I got you." she pleads.

"No, the floor is moving." he iterates.

"Where are your keys?" Milan asks.

He doesn't answer so she reaches into his left front pocket and fishes them out. She tosses the keys to Ariel and tells her to pull Lock's car around to the back of the building and they will take him out through the kitchen. Once the car is in position both girls shuffle Lock out the back and dump him into his own back seat. Milan drives and Ariel rides shotgun to take Lock home. Attica, Schemer and News are still lingering out front waiting for Lock to exit, and with Castle already in the wind, their frustration only grows.

They pull up to Lock's house and he is barely coherent. He is not a heavy drinker at all, and never does any drugs, so mixing alcohols all night combined with being roofied has Lock worse for wear. Milan uses Lock's key to unlock his door, and leaves it open to make it easier to lug him across the threshold. Milan and Ariel each put their head under an arm and struggle mightily to get him up the steps and into the house. His feet drag so badly that his Wotherspoon's are scuffed beyond repair.

Reena and Monae are tucked away in a booth at the diner waiting for Lock to arrive. All night diners are a NJ staple and it is common practice for hundreds of people to show up to eat after the club. The place is not super packed on this occasion so Monae and Reena already have their food. Reena ordered pancakes and bacon while Monae went for a cheese omelette with home fries and turkey sausage.
"I wanted to wait for Lock to get here before I started eating, but I'm hungry girl." Reena proclaims.

Already three bites into her omelette Monae quips
"He'll be OK."

" So let me tell you about my little soap opera this past week." Reena says.

After pausing for a second to focus on cutting her pancakes into perfectly symmetrical pieces, she continues.
"Lock just busts into my house the other day and said that he wants us to be together."

"What's wrong with that? From what I know y'all are like soulmates anyway, right?" Monae asks.

"I mean, I'm sure it could work. I mean, nobody knows me like him, and of course I love him; we've been close since we rode big wheels. Love and in love are two different things though and I don't know if he's really in love with me. Plus, why would he just spring that on me like that?" Reena replies.

Then Monae asks,
"So what did you do?"

"I told him that he couldn't just rush in like that and expect an answer. I think that pissed him off a little bit. It's crazy though because I was just about to finally give in and give Castle some attention and Lock literally walks in that very second and said what he said."

Monae's mouth hangs wide open, then she asks,
"So Castle was already there when Lock showed up?"

Reena twist her lip up on one side and raises an eyebrow while slightly dipping her head forward
"Girl, yes."
Then she goes on further to say
"Like, why is this happening though? Lock has been so close to me forever, and I can't lie, I've thought about us being together a thousand times, but I always just push the idea out of my head. On the other hand, I can tell by the way Castle looks at me that there's some kind of feeling there. It's just different. The bad thing is no matter who I pick, somebody is gonna be mad at me, and our little clique might be ruined forever. I should just run away. I never asked for any of this."

After all of that, Monae responds
"Just follow your heart."

"Gee thanks." Reena sarcastically quips.

She calls Lock's phone for about the tenth time and he doesn't answer.
"He's not answering. Come on girl, we're leaving." Reena tells Monae.

~

Milan and Ariel lay Lock on his bed and undress him down to his boxers and wife beater. Ariel is intrigued by his bedroom. His bed is huge-a California King that sits high from the floor. One entire wall is custom wallpaper barring the image floor-to-ceiling of the late, great Aaliyah. A 60-inch flat screen is mounted on another wall with a soundbar and surround sound hookup. His closet door is open and shoeboxes touch the ceiling. Once Lock is all set, Milan gives Ariel one last run through. She tells Ariel,

"OK, I'm about to leave. Don't forget to take the pics and send them to me. Don't fuck him, but act like you did. Stay here until he wakes up, and tell him that he was great and all that type of bullshit."

"Bitch I don't even have my car, I ain't going nowhere. Just make sure you come pick me up in the morning, and how can I fuck this nigga anyway with him over here knocked out?" Ariel replies.

"Text me in the morning. Don't forget to take those pics."

Lock wakes up around 11AM and has his grogginess snatched away as he realizes Ariel laying next to him. She is already awake and is watching the movie "Paid In Full". Right about the time that Mitch tells Ace "I'm thinking more like ten days," Lock is asking Ariel,
    "How did we get here?"

"You brought me here, silly!" she replies.

With a look of utter disbelief on his face, he asks
    "Did we..?"
Before he could finish the question she cuts him off.
    "Don't tell me you don't remember."

She already texted Milan to tell her that Lock is awake, she also sent the selfies of her in Lock's bed as he slept like a baby next to her. His face is clear in every picture. She rolls over on her side to face Lock and put her palm on his forearm.
    "My girl is about to come get me. You're gonna call me though, right?"

Milan texts back "Pulling up in a sec."

Lock asks her
    "Who drove here, me or you?"

Ariel replies
    "You did my car is still in Philly. Plus how would I know how to get here?"

Still puzzled, Lock states
    "I guess."

No sooner than that there's a knock at his bedroom door then it instantaneously opens. Gliding through the door with a McDonald's bag containing a fresh order of hotcakes is Reena.

Chapter 12

NO CHURCH IN THE WILD

Nearly on the outskirts of town, though not quite as far out as the high school, a concrete and rock driveway stretches a couple hundred yards away from the road. Settled on the other side is the Salem City Pool. The grounds consist of three swimming areas, each one larger than the last. The front booth serves triple purposes as also a guard shack and concession stand. Winding to the left and right are separate entrances leading to respective changing houses for males and females where the smell of the chlorine water that soaks the concrete is only accented by the aroma of freshly cut grass. On the other side lies a concrete oasis where Salem City kids spend countless hours practically sunrise to sunset. As a child Attica was no different. He found his way to the pool whenever he could afford the small entrance fee, and many days stayed until it closed for the evening.

Most days followed a strict routine as far as trips to the pool were concerned. Attica would meet with a group of friends, as little as three and as many as nine or ten, around 9AM every morning. After the initial rendezvous, the group would travel to John Fenwick School for one of the many free breakfast programs located throughout the city. Since often times they were not all coming from the same streets or neighborhoods, the school was the best place to eat at because it was perfectly placed on the route to the final destination. Most members of the group owned bikes, and those who did not usually received rides either on the handlebars or standing on the back pegs. Attica loved his bike, it wasn't brand new-it was something straight from "The Island of Misfit Toys". He had actually put it together himself from the parts of several broken bikes left abandoned or thrown into the trash. The final touch that he placed on his Frankenstein carriage was an artistically done spray paint job. He painted his bike red and black, the same colors worn by Michael Jordan and the Chicago Bulls. He used masking tape to form straight break lines and spent hours turning his creation into a masterpiece. When he was finished, no one in town had a bike like his. It looked expensive, but costed him next to nothing. After meeting with his crew and scarfing down the selected free breakfast of the day, the gang would head to the pool for the free swim which lasted from 10AM until noon. The morning sessions were rarely packed, which meant that the boys could partake in activities that are not permitted when the pools are filled with people. Games like tackle football, where the runner is not considered down until he is completely dunked underwater. Another of the popular contests were one on one duels where water is splashed ferociously, usually with an open hand and a hard forward thrusting motion until one person backs down or surrenders under a constant liquid barrage. At noon when the morning session ended, they would find their way back to John Fenwick School for the free lunch program. After free sandwiches, milk, chips and apple juice it was time to head back to the pool. Sometimes if they ate too quickly they would make it back well before 1PM and would have to wait outside in a line until they were permitted to enter. This time, however, admittance was not free. Sometimes Attica had money, other times he did not. There were many instances where his friends would band together to pay for him. It was never a huge issue between them, it would take away from the fun if someone was missing.

The sun rises and falls repeatedly, each day fresh and new even when carried out repetitiously, until the constantly growing path known as memory lumps each separate day into a jumble of experiences unhinged from any particular solar cycle in one's ability to recall. Days run together, and are often not remembered as one from the next unless a major event occurs and seers it into memory. For Attica, one such day was after a free morning session at the pool. A day that began like they all did with breakfast and a bit of rough-house play in the water. After the morning session was over Attica took his time getting dressed, mainly because he wanted to dry his feet well. He always hates the feeling of trying to put his socks on when his feet were still wet. It was tough pulling them up against moist skin, and it felt mushy once he would put his sneakers on. The only other option was to put his sneakers on without socks, but then the water from his wet shorts would run down his leg and directly into his shoes which was just as bad or worse. Attica and his young friends cracked jokes and stung each other with the tips of rolled up towels as they got dressed for their excursion to enjoy a free lunch. Most of the kids at the time would hold each end of their towels and swing them in a front to back causing the towel to twist up, creating a tip which when perfectly flipped out sting the skin like a bullwhip. Attica learned a new method of neatly folding the towel which seemed to give it a little extra pop. He put his device to the test while chasing his friend Trav halfway around the pool grounds after Trav stung him in the back because he felt that Attica was holding the group up by taking too much time to dry his precious feet. Still to this point, the day had been unremarkable. As they made their way through the winding change house and past the booth they spilled into the parking lot and over to the bike rack. At that moment Attica's heart plummeted to his freshly dried feet. His bike was gone! When dollars are scarce they tend to be rationed out begrudgingly, and a chain with a lock was something that Attica just could not afford. Attica felt such a huge sense of loss, followed almost immediately by a burning rage. Who took it? Where did they go? Attica's friends tried to calm him, and promised to help him look for the bike after lunch. Trav gave Attica a ride on his handlebars to the school where upon arrival they see Attica's bike leaning amongst a pile of bikes belonging to kids already inside the cafeteria. Relieved, Attica doesn't attempt to find out who took it, he just calmly picked it up and placed it in between the separate pile that his friends began to make. They put it in the middle, therefore if someone were to attempt to take the bike again, they would have to first remove three other bikes in the process. Crisis averted as Attica had his prize back in possession. After lunch the band flew back to the pool and continued on having a great time.

The next day, lightning struck twice. "How could I be so stupid?" Attica thought to himself. He placed his bike in a position on the bike rack that would be visible from inside of the pool area, but it was impossible to keep a watchful eye while diving, splashing and playing. Attica was absolutely livid, and as he rode to the school on Trav's handlebars for the second time his embarrassment fueled his anger. They again reached the school and there laid Attica's bike. He was slightly happy, but so enraged that he found no peace. He didn't even eat that day, he just sat there waiting for lunch to adjourn so that he could find out who it was that stole his bike. He wasn't sure that the same culprit was responsible for both days, but in his mind they would have to fight for both thefts. As the kids began to file out, some on bikes and some on foot, Attica stood by the window, still inside the building. He kept his eyes locked on his bike and waited astutely until he saw a boy named Steph walk over to the bike, stand it upright, then sit on the seat. Before Steph could position his feet to pedal away, Attica jetted out of the building placing himself directly in front of Steph's intended path. With his left hand Attica gripped the handlebar and said to Steph,
    "Yo, this is my bike."

Attica was nervous because Steph was a year older than him and also outweighed him by at least twenty pounds. Attica made up his mind that if it came to it, he had to attack first. Steph said,

"Nah man, I got this bike from…"

Before he could complete his sentence, Attica with his left hand still clinging to the handlebar balled his free right hand into a fist and fired an overhand punch with bad intentions. The strike landed flush on Steph's cheek just in front of his ear with such power that it sounded like a smack. The force knocked Steph back, but his loose basketball shorts snagged the bike's seat causing him to stumble in his retreat while somewhat dragging the bike with him as Attica continued to hold on. Attica then released his grasp as he pushed the front of the bike to the ground and sped around it to meet Steph as he fell. Attica knew that he couldn't let up. If he let Steph get his feet back under him the tables could easily turn. As Steph stumbled to the ground Attica expedited the process with a stiff push and mounted him in full guard. Attica showered down a flurry of lefts and rights until Steph could do nothing but cover his face and cower. Attica then rose, pick his bike up high above his head and slammed it onto Steph where he lay in the grass. He then retrieved the bike and parted, but not before one last swift kick to the guy for good measure. Trav and the rest of Attica's friends were stunned. Fights happened a lot, but never before had a member of their small fraternity taken an older kid to task with such authority. Attica didn't have to worry about anyone else stealing his bike. There were probably kids who would have beaten Attica in a fight, but the word was out that he would fight relentlessly and there were much easier bikes to target-Attica's was safe. It taught him a valuable lesson that he still lives by: sometimes to get respect, you have to make an example of people. There's a saying that goes "Once you're tagged lame, the game is follow the leader." Meaning that once a person is perceived as weak, people will take advantage every chance afforded them. Attica feels that the only way to end the thought of such a thing is through quick, harsh violence.

***

After Castle managed to slither away from the party, Attica took it as a slap in the face. After all, he directly told Castle not to leave before meeting with him. Attica along with News and Schemer waited outside the club on the off chance that Castle was still inside and had somehow managed to get caught up with wrapping up the party. If Castle was not to be found, then Lock was to be a consolation. However, in his inebriated state he was hauled through the back door and on his way over the Ben

Franklin Bridge before Attica deemed the stakeout fruitless. By the time the trio reaches Salem, Attica is fuming mad. The empty ride home was reminiscent of his time on Trav's handlebars years earlier, each passing minute one part gasoline and one part oxygen to the already potent flame that is Attica's temper. Once inside News' apartment Attica tells him,

"Find Castle and knock his shit off!"

News responds

"I think we should give it a few weeks. Too many bodies too close together. That ain't a good look."

Attica raises his intensity a notch as he yells,

"Fuck that shit! This nigga must think I'm a joke! Fly his shit ASAP!"

Schemer jumps in and says,

"That's a bad idea. I mean, I get it. I get what you mean about the whole reputation thing. But nobody knows the nigga owes you money."

"I don't got a problem taking him out, but we gotta give it some time. I can deal with these local cops. Even if the state comes in, all they gonna do is put the state boys on patrol, but they won't do no investigations. If the Feds come in bro, they gonna nail everybody to the cross. They don't even prove it either. If they think you did it, they just lie until you get convicted. We don't need that shit bro." News inserts.

Attica replies without wasting a second.

"I ain't trying to wait, fuck that!"

Then he looks over at Schemer and says

"And it ain't about if people know-I know!"

News sighs and slightly hangs his head as Attica's stubbornness has a tiring affect. He then says to Attica,

"Real talk bro, you know I ain't scared of shit in these streets. Even thorough niggas gotta know when to chill out though. You been locked up more than me, but I know the Feds better than you. I was out here with mad niggas who got caught up in Fed cases. My boy Reef from Strawberry Mansion got bagged over there in Philly. When they got him in the interrogation room they said to him 'We got you with one key, but we know you did ten, so we're gonna charge you with ten.'

What kinda shit is that? Then they asked him about some nigga from another neighborhood, Kensington I think he said. So he keeps telling them 'Look, I don't know this muthafucka!' Then one of the agents slid him a surveillance picture and said 'Is this you and him?' He looked and the pic and said 'Well I guess so.'

All three men laugh a little, and News continues,

"Real talk, he really didn't know the dude though. He was walking past and saw a few guys that he knew standing there, so you know how it is, he shook everybody's hand that was standing there just out of respect. These bitch ass Feds took the pic as he's shaking the boy's hand and used it as part of the case they built for a conspiracy. Reef got twenty years and part of it was for shaking a nigga's hand that he didn't even know. He ain't even know this nigga's name. That's the shit we gonna be up against, and it ain't even like these little niggas is a threat, this is some kiddie shit to me."

"Man, fuck the Feds!" Attica screams. "Get this bitch ass nigga tonight. I'm tired of playing games. Knock his head off and we'll get the money from his square ass friend. That's it!"

"You're tripping bro. That's not smart." Schemer says to Attica.

"Get the fuck outta here with that intellectual bullshit, Schemer. All that smart shit go out the window sometimes. You act real fucking soft sometimes, and you better straighten the fuck up or stay from around me." Attica barks back at Schemer.

Schemer sucks his teeth then inhales deeply and mumbles under his breath,
    "Whatever nigga."

"What was that!? You got something to say!?" Attica yells.

News steps in and says
    "Y'all pipe down. I'm about to go change my clothes and I'll go look for him real quick. It's late as hell so he probably won't be out, but I'll see if I can catch him going to the crib. I'm laying low for a while after this though. The block is gonna be hot as fish grease after another body so I'm chilling."

News exits to prepare and Schemer follows moments behind. As News searches his drawers and closet for the right clothes to wear, Schemer tries to reason with him.

"News, you know this ain't the right move. You gotta talk some sense into this dude. Not only is he gonna make it hot out here, but then he won't even get whatever money he wanted if Castle dies."

"We'll just make the other boy pay." News replies.

"Come on bruh, it's bad business and you know it. I'm all about getting money, but I see six different ways for this to backfire and only one way that it works."

As News gathers his clothes, he reaches into a separate drawer and produces a gunmetal gray Desert Eagle. It's the biggest handgun that Schemer has ever seen in his life.
"What the fuck are you in the NRA or some shit? I never see you with the same gun twice."
"Nah bro" News replies "We started doing this thing where we swap them with other hoods. At first it was just Salem and Bridgeton swapping with Camden and Philly, but that's too close so now we send them to New York and Boston. I know some people up in Brownsville and Roxbury, so if they put in work and need to ship a gun out they send it down here, and we can do the same. It's way better than throwing them in the river and taking a loss like we used to do."

"Y'all treat murder like it's the stock market or something." Schemer states.

"Them muthafuckas are way worse than us-they rob, steal and kill every day, and they never go to jail," News responds.

"Give me a chance to set this thing straight before you go handle this shit bro." Schemer pleads.

"You know that ain't how this shit works. Just pray that he ain't out there and go talk to Attica while I'm gone." News suggests.

Schemer whines,
"Man you see that he's not trying to listen to nothing. That kinda attitude can get us all jammed up. I know you ain't scared? You gotta talk to him, he'll listen to you."

"The fuck you mean scared? Nigga I ain't scared of shit." News replies as he turns and takes a step in Schemer's direction.

"My bad, I didn't mean it like that. I'll talk to him." Schemer says with his hands in the air.

News barks "Yeah that's what I thought."

As News tucks the hand cannon into his belt line he says to Schemer,

"I was kinda with you on this for a minute, but don't get too smart for your own good."

News sets up not far from Castle's house. Across the street and a few doors down in between two houses, he lies in wait for his potential sacrifice. News likes to approach on an angle-it confuses the victim, not giving them a clear path to run without remaining in the line of fire. He's calm but uneasy, nothing new for a Serengeti cat crouched low to the ground in a patch of high brush. He continues to wait until he finally decides that after ten minutes more he will retire and hunt another day.

That very instant a car pulls up. It's not Castle's car, but it parks very close to the front of his house. News slowly reaches into his hoodie's pouch pocket. His previously unworn sweatshirt has been customized with the same slight rips at the edges of the pocket. He grips the handle of his firearm and watches intently while creeping forward. He observes a woman emerging from the driver seat. He can't identify her as the streetlight nearest to where the vehicle is parked seems to be broken. The male passenger stands but bends down to grab something out of the car. By this time News is already in full stride, not running but more of the extremely brisk walk of a serial killer in a slasher film. As the young woman notices the dark figure zeroing in on them she screams and drops her keys. Even though she already locked her door she pulls the handle voraciously before sliding to the ground in terror. News makes it to the other side of the car to find his potential victim curled into a ball lightly whimpering with his fingers locked behind his head.

"Turn over!" News yells.

News views himself as honorable, and never once shot a man in his back unless fired upon first and the initial aggressor ran away. News is a master at the element of surprise, but never a man with his back turned. He gives the man a slight kick and says to him sternly

"Castle, turn over! Look at me!"

He steps back slightly as to avoid blood spatter and puts the slightest bit of pressure on the trigger-not enough to fire, just enough to meet resistance. This will allow for a lightning fast shot. No sooner than News makes his backward motion, the woman now standing in the street on the other side of the car rips through the chilly silence of the night with a long, drawn-out blood curdling,

"Stopppp!"

Chapter 13

THE MESSAGE

....

Salem is almost totally surrounded by water. On the far end of 7th Street where Lock grew up flows The Mannington Creek, a tributary of The Salem River which in turn draws from The Delaware. Lock spent many childhood hours down by the water. There was an entrance on the other side of Hubbell Avenue, which is the next street over from 7th, where train tracks led through a strip of land with water flowing on both sides. Aside from the creek, this was also the spot where many young artists bombed their first train cars. Bombing is a term used to describe graffiti art, and in those days Salem had an abundance of artistic talent. Some hailed the works as masterpieces where others decried it as vandalism. Preventative steps were taken, none seemed to ever prove successful. Some days Reena would accompany Lock on his outings by the water. For years Lock tried unsuccessfully to teach Reena how to skip rocks. She totally threw like a girl and never garnered any success. Lock, however, was a master of the sidearm sling. To be a great rock skipper is to understand angles. The rock must skim across the top of the water, so the perfect angle means more skips for any particular stone. Flat stones skip the best, but Lock got so good that he took pride in skipping any shape. The contest is won by the person who can get a single throw to touch the top of the water the most times before eventually entering the water for good. Great throws grow harder and harder to count as the rock begins to tap the water in rapid succession towards the end of its run. Lock held his record at 32 skips which was far more than any of his friends. 32 more than Reena ever accomplished.

Occasionally people would fish at the creek as well, and Lock tried his hat at teaching Reena how to catch fish one Summer. He did most of the work as she was dead set against touching any worms. She would have much rather thrown her hook into the water baitless before she ever came in contact with those squiggly vessels of terror. She did cast her own line into the water and one day managed to catch the biggest fish that either of them had ever seen. Her line began to tug which sent her into a dance of excitement that more resembled jumping up and down while screaming a bunch of gibberish. She refused to let Lock help her reel it in, so he coached her step by step through the battle, barking instructions like Burgess Meredith. With as much sway and drama as a Balboa title fight, Reena emerged victorious, finally landing a knockout by plucking her foe from the watery ring. She then refused to touch the fish once it was out of the water as the carp's violent flapping more than petrified her and she would not come close. Still, Reena holds bragging rights for owning the biggest haul, while Lock has always tried to steal as much credit as possible.

The only lie that Lock ever told Reena was born of an incident that occurred at that very place near the water. Late September days in New Jersey are complex to say the least. Early mornings are chilly and often jacket weather, by the afternoon hours the sun beams down with the year's last efforts at sweltering oppression. A bit of a reminder that Summer is the object in the rearview mirror, still closer than it appears. After a Friday football practice, Lock and a few of his friends Juice, D-Rock and Steelo decided to go down by the trains to smoke. Their real names were Jimmy, Deonte and Ricky but this was freshman year, and it was super uncool to not have a nickname. Lock didn't smoke, but that never stopped him from hanging with his friends who did. Castle promised to meet them there but had fallen off of the radar after walking his new girlfriend home. The four adolescents climbed up the ladder of a detached train car and held a normal teenage conversation as they sat atop. Nearly a half hour passes before a commotion can be heard over by the water. Five boys stood there in a precarious huddle. Even at a distance, their body language screamed of confrontation. The conversation on the train slammed to an immediate halt as everyone focused their attention on the potential quarrel looming beneath. The kettle came to boil as two of the boys squared off in guarded stances. As Lock looked more closely it became clear that the chubby light skinned figure dancing in a boxer's circle was Mike. Lock had known Mike since he was a baby being as though he is Reena's little brother. He shifted his attention to Mike's opponent. It was Corey, another kid from the other side of 7th Street that Lock had known forever. Once it became apparent that fisticuffs would ensue, the other three boys hurried from the train to witness. Lock stayed perched on the iron horse having made up his mind that as long as the fight remained fair he would not intervene.

One of the greatest rivalries in South Jersey is Salem and longstanding arch nemesis, Penns Grove. If the feuding cities decided to produce badminton teams the tickets would sell out in minutes and the crowd would be hostile. The afternoon after Mike's fight Salem played Penns Grove on their home field. The bleachers were filled to the brim and the entire area surrounding the field was standing room only. Like always, the game was a mini fashion show and everyone who was anyone came looking less than perfect. Lock, Castle and Juice posted up on Salem's side of the field right by the entrance. This way they would see all of the girls from Penns Grove as they entered. Just before halftime Reena, Milan and a group of three other girls pass by on their way to the concession stand. Rarely ever had Lock and Reena passed each other without speaking and true to form she stopped for a second to chat with him.

"Hey" she said to him.
"Hey, what's up?" Lock said right back.

"Nothing much. Hey, Mikey got into a fight yesterday and ended up having to go to the hospital. He busted his mouth open pretty bad. Did you hear anything about that?" she asked.

With his eyes glued to the field, never looking Reena in the face Lock replied "Nah, that's crazy. Is he good though?"

"Yeah, he should be fine as far as I know. He's lumped up though. Let me know what you find out," Reena stated as she began to step away at a faster pace than normal to catch up with her friends who had only waited a few seconds before creeping away.
"I got you," Lock replied as she scampered away.

Lock had never lied to Reena before, but he knew that as a girl she would never truly understand how guys operate. He knew that she would have expected him to help her brother or at least stop the fight. Lock felt that stopping the fight would have put a target on Mike's back and he would only have to fight that much harder the next time. There was nothing wrong with earning stripes and respect, but most girls seem to never see it that way. For teenage boys, fistfights are a neighborhood's version of dialysis. It gets rid of the bad blood and more other than not the two combatants are friends again within a week. Girls, on the other hand, hold grudges for years, and once blows are thrown most friendships are completely unsalvageable. Lock knew Reena's reactions before they would occur so in the seconds that it took for him to deny hearing or seeing anything he had already played out in his mind her overblown response to him being there. Before he could blink the "Nah" part of his response had snuck out of his mouth without effort or permission. He felt bad for not telling her, but he quickly concluded that it was insignificant and that since Mike was fine the whole thing was water under the bridge.

Friday right before last period always felt different for Lock. There was an electricity in the air that could not be denied. Maybe it was the barely contained jubilee of the weekend on the horizon. Whatever it was, it was always real to Lock. As the students swam through the halls wearing brighter smiles than at any other point of the week, Lock noticed Reena walking his way yet she was not smiling at all. It reminded him of the scene from the movie "A Bronx Tale" where Cee notices the guy not smiling in the crowd, but couldn't reach Sonny in time to stop the guy from shooting him. The closer she came was as if Lock could hear her feet pounding the floor. The lack of emotion on her face amplified his jitters as she drew closer. Once they were standing face to face she proceeded to stare at him awkwardly for about five seconds, almost as if she were expecting him to say exactly what she wanted to hear. Finally, she began to throw a series of half fisted punches to Lock's chest as she screams at him
    "You were there! You were there and you didn't tell me!?"

Completely taken aback, Lock said nothing at first. He grabbed Reena by the wrists and in a quiet voice he said,
    "Let's talk about this later."

Reena would have none of it and she continued to attempt to free her hands in order to get in a few more shoves.

    "Don't talk to me!" she screamed as she stormed away.

The entire hallway stopped to witness the altercation and Lock stood there just as embarrassed as if he had walked through naked. Not many in the school ever believed that they were not dating, and what could have been misconstrued as a lover's quarrel only added fuel to the rumors. During last period, Lock could think of nothing other than how upset Reena was with him. D-Rock accidentally spilled the beans to Reena the period before. He had no idea that Lock told Reena that he knew nothing about the fight, so as he filled her in on the details of the brawl, he mentioned that Lock could validate his truth because he too saw the whole thing. She was so upset that she left her books at school and turned down several rides home, choosing instead to walk and calm herself down. She did not take his calls all weekend but eventually showed up at his door willing to hash it out. They talked for hours about their differing stances and finally managed to patch things up. Ultimately, Lock pinky promised and swore on a stack of bibles that he would never lie to Reena again. She accepted his apology but only if it came with a cheesesteak and fries. An inexpensive olive branch helped to repair such a valuable trust.

***

Floating like a skylark through Lock's bedroom door, Reena never expected to see a woman lying there in his bed. As her eyes scour the room a million thoughts and emotions rush in like unblocked linebackers attacking a vulnerable quarterback. The song of the skylark abruptly ended by a blast to the chest, ripping it from the sky and sending it crashing to the uncompromising ground. She notices an empty condom wrapper amongst a pile of crumpled clothes on the woman's side of the bed, which is closest to her as she stands in the doorway. On the nightstand next to a half-empty bottle of Deer Park sit two earrings and a bangle. Reena doesn't look the lady in the face as she pans her line of site through her and over to Lock. Aside from the tiny slices creeping past the curtains, the only light in the room is flooding in behind Reena's back at the open door plus the flickering glow of the television screen. Lock has not seen such a look on Reena's face since that day in the hallway of Salem High. Today, however, there is a pain in her eyes not present before. The meeting of their eyes is awkward and uncomfortable. Lock wants desperately to look away but some cruel outside force will not allow him to tear his eyes from hers. If ever silence made a noise it is happening, reaching a crescendo when broken by the words,
"Hi, I'm Ariel."
Ariel reaches out her hand in a friendly gesture offering a handshake even as Reena is feet away from the foot of the king size bed and not nearly close enough to engage.

"Is this your sister Lock?" she asks in a syrupy voice that usually begets violence in a situation like this. Even as Ariel speaks, Reena's eyes are fixed upon Lock and the McDonald's bag that she is holding slips from her fingertips. The plastic cup of orange juice explodes as it hits the floor jarring Reena from her trance. Without a word she turns and walks away. After a few steps, she breaks into a jog in an attempt to hurry to her car in case she fails at holding back the tears striving to well at the corners of her eyes. Lock leaps from his bed in pursuit, but is impeded by the puddle of orange juice soaking his socks as he races to the door. He hurries to peel the knitted boots from his feet and jumps into a pair of basketball shorts taken from his dresser drawer, he follows behind Reena only to find that he is too late as he sees only the rear of her car speeding away.

Re-entering his bedroom, he finds Ariel rushing to dress and gather her things. She says to Lock,
"My girl is about to come pick me up, she's almost here."

Emotionless, Lock simply replies
"Aight."

She walks over to him, puts her arm around his neck and kisses him on the cheek.
"Call me soon, OK?" she says to him before letting go.

"I will. I'm still kinda confused on how we got here, so we definitely need to talk again. Are you sure you gotta go right now?" he says.

"Yeah baby, I'm sorry. She just called me and said that she was almost here. She's probably already out front. I'll text you when I get home."

Lock walks her to the front door and closes it behind her. As he walks back to his dark bedroom it feels like he is entering a sarcophagus. He steps around the citric puddle without an inkling of a thought about getting it up. The look on Reena's face is seared into his conscience and he doesn't know how to turn this one around. He has not even begun to confront the situation with Castle which is a separate but equal train wreck. His life is in a tailspin and he lays there in the dark all but wishing that he was dead.

Outside, Ariel doesn't see Milan's car, so she calls her to get a fix on her location.
"Where you at?" she asks.

"I'm right around the corner, I couldn't pull up in front of his door. Just come around the corner, I'm right here."

Ariel walks up and gets into the passenger seat of Milan's charcoal gray Nissan Maxima. She says to Milan,

"Damn girl, why didn't you tell me that he was gonna have somebody coming by. Luckily she didn't wanna fight 'cause I wasn't even dressed."

Milan responds,

"I didn't know. I was on my way to get you and I saw her pull up so I just kept right on driving."

Milan giggles a little and then asks Ariel,

"So what happened? What did she say to you?"

Ariel says to her,

"Nothing. She didn't say a word. She looked like she was getting ready to cry and ran out."

"Well that worked out better than the pictures that I was gonna send her." Milan added.

"Girl, you owe me extra now. I don't even know why I said I would do this anyway. What if he was crazy or something?" Ariel asked.

"Please girl, Lock is the last dude you gotta worry about being crazy, he's nice. I knew you was gonna be safe the whole time. He ain't even the type that would try to force you if you said no or something like that, and he definitely wouldn't put his hands on you. He don't even act conceited like a lot of guys do if they're getting money or got a little name out here." Milan adds.

"Well if he's so nice, then why'd you wanna get him caught up like that?" Ariel asks.

"It ain't even about him. Really, it's not about Reena either. It's just kinda complicated and a lot to explain. I'll break it all down for you one day." Milan tells Ariel.

"OK, well just make sure you come through with those names for me, 'cause I definitely need that bread. How'd you learn how to do that anyway?" Ariel asks.

Milan replies,

"My cousin taught me. She works at the nursing home so she got access to a lot of social security numbers. A lot of those old people don't file their taxes so she wrote down a bunch of names and numbers, then her and her boyfriend filed them all on TurboTax. Once they went through they brought me in on it and taught me."

"That's so crazy girl! Well definitely remember my three names like you promised." Ariel says.

"I got you" Milan replies. "I gotta swing past my house first and then I'll take you to your car. We can get something to eat on the way."

Ariel says to her
"Yeah, that sounds good."

After leaving Lock's house, Reena did not want to go home so she drove around without direction. Her first destination was Milan's place, but she noticed that her car was not there so she drove past without stopping. She tightly grips the steering wheel with her hands at the eleven and one o'clock positions, only the purr of the engine and wind resistance hum away at the quietness. There is a lump in her throat that causes a pinch more pain each time she forces it down with a hard gulp of air. Her pride is like the mighty Hoover dam holding her tears at bay. At the last second, before it is too late to make the left turn, she settles on going to Monae's house. She parks her car, and before exiting she pushes to collect herself. She puts on the pair of sunglasses that were resting in the console, a large lens pair by Dior that she hopes will mask the turmoil that her face most surely explains. She sends Monae a text that reads "Out front. Headed to your door." and after a few deep breaths, she exits the car. She waits at Monae's door for less than thirty seconds, fidgety, tapping the sides of her thighs with her open hands. Monae answers and says to her
"Hey, come in."

No sooner than Reena breaches the doorway the levies relent, and tears spill down her face. Monae grabs her by the shoulders from behind and asks
"Oh my god, what's wrong Reena."

In full cry, Reena is powerless to mutter a clear word nor does she try. Monae guides her through the walkway and over to the couch where Reena withers into a ball. Monae sits next to her and lifts Reena's head high enough to place it in her lap. She tries again to ask what is bothering her but Reena just cries. Monae strokes her fingers through Reena 's hair in a motion from front to back while trying to console her. For the next ten minutes, Monae makes not a sound, rubbing Reena's head as she lay there with her hands in the sleeves of her shirt and covering her face. Finally, she lifts her head and sits upright. She stares at the floor for a few seconds before finally looking Monae in her face. She feels more tears may be coming so she slaps her hands down beside her on the couch cushion hoping that the release of energy will stop them in their path. Monae puts her hand on top of Reena's and asks her,

"Do you wanna talk about it?

She reaches over to the end table and grabs a box of Kleenex. She hands them to Reena and says,

"Here, I'll be right back."

She walks to the kitchen and fills a kettle with water, she places it on the stovetop and grabs a mug from the cabinet. She takes two teabags and places them into the mug then adding a few spoonfuls of sugar. She finally heads back into the main room to talk with Reena while the water boils.

Finally poised enough to speak, Reena says,

"So tell me how I never heard from Lock last night, and when I woke up I didn't have any texts or missed calls from him. I wasn't even mad though. So I get up and I stop by McDonald's 'cause he loves the pancakes and I figured we could talk while he ate. I was feeling really good this morning for some reason and I thought that maybe it was because we had such a good time last night. You know I don't go out much, and it was just a good time, no drama, no fights or shooting. Something told me to go check on Lock so I grabbed the food and headed over. I walk in his room and he's lying there in the bed with a naked girl. I couldn't tell if I was sad or mad. I literally couldn't even talk."

Monae listens intently with her mouth wide open. She asks Reena

"So what did you do?"

"I just left, I wasn't playing when I said that I couldn't talk. I can't believe that he would do that. Especially after he came to my house claiming that he loves me so much and that he wanted us to be together. I should've never got my hopes up." Reena replies.

"How'd you get all the way in the house in the first place?" Monae asks.

"I have a key. Lock gave it to me before he left for school so I could check on his Grand Pop from time to time. I was expecting to open the door and see him still asleep, or something like that. Instead, some silly chick is laying there trying to smile all in my face and acting all fake and bubbly. I should have dragged her out of that bed by her stupid looking hair," Reena says.

"Girl, you're always talking about how you don't fight," Monae inserts.

"I don't, but not because I can't," Reena replies.
Then with her head hanging low, she rests her hands in the seam where her thighs are touching and inhales deeply. As she exhales her shoulders drop in pity. She raises her head and begins to say,
"I just..." but before she could finish tears again descend from her eyes only to be impeded as she dabs them away with her sleeve. Monae gets up from her seat and says to Reena,
"Hold on real quick, let me check on this water." She makes her way into the kitchen and though the water in the kettle hasn't reached enough of a boil to create a whistle, it is more than hot enough for a cup of tea. She pours the water into the mug that she prepared minutes earlier, then places the steaming ceramic inside of a paper towel and walks it out, handing it to Reena as she sits there trying mightily to get her emotions in check. Reena accepts Monae's offering, softly thanking her for her kindness. She holds the mug at its bottom with her right hand while with her left swirling the contents with the spoon in a counterclockwise circular motion. The familiar clang of the utensil meeting the inner edge of the china slows to a cease as Reena commences to speak.
"I'm sorry that I just showed up and dumped all of this on you. I really didn't wanna go to my parents' house though."

Monae responds,
"You are fine, it's not a problem at all. You can always come by if you need to talk. Honestly, you can come by if you need to cry, curse or scream. Trust me I know how it is. I've been through so much with these sorry behind dudes myself that I understand what you're going through. I know that we don't hang together a lot, but you have always been straight up with me and you're a good person. Anybody who doesn't see that, it's their loss."

She lightens the mood a little bit by saying to Reena,

"Plus girl, you can get any guy you want. You look like you should be in Destiny's Child, and you don't got no kids! Winner, winner!"

Reena chuckles and puts her hand over her face as she smiles. Reena then says to Monae,
"I really appreciate you, and yeah you're right, we should hang out more. It's probably my fault that we didn't. You hang out with Milan and I do too, but we manage to not hang out with each other. That doesn't even make sense. It's just so much I'm dealing with right now. I'm trying to finish school and get back on track which you already know, and I was doing OK, everything was regular. The crazy thing about this whole situation with Lock is that it came from nowhere, and I was seriously about to give it a shot with Castle."

Monae's face lights up with surprise!
"What?" she says in a long drawn out manner.

"It's so hard to explain." Reena says.
She sips a spoonful of tea before delving in deeper.
"So, me and Lock never dated or anything. I'm sure we both thought about it a lot, and there was this one time where we probably almost took it there but we never did. He has really just been my friend my whole life. He never really likes any of the guys that I talk to, but he doesn't make me feel bad for dating. I honestly think he would flip out if I talk to Castle, and now Castle is gonna be heartbroken if I choose Lock. How did I even get in this situation? It's like I'm not committed to either one of them technically, but still forbidden from each of them because of the other. The three of us have been hanging together since the 1st grade and I don't know how to get it back to normal. I almost just wanna run away."

"That's way too deep for me. I don't know what to tell you right now. I have to think about it some more before I can give you a good answer" Monae replies.

"I know I can't deal with Lock after this. I would expect that from some guy that I don't know, but not the one who waited for three hours to get Omarion's autograph for me and he hated B2K."

Monae jumps in to ask
"He did what?"

Smiling, Reena replies

"Girl, don't judge me, I used to absolutely love Omarion when I was little. Don't act like I'm the only one!"

She looks up to the ceiling as if she is pondering and says to Monae,

"What was I saying? Oh yeah, I just can't understand him. He didn't have to start this, we were fine as just friends. I don't even have words for him right now. I know I'm not perfect, but I'm a good person. I was minding my own business and he comes playing with my emotions just to walk all over them. Why do guys always do stuff like this? I think I'm more hurt over the whole situation than just him. It Lock, it's Castle, it's all of the stuff that I have going on in my life. I think this happening just sent it over the top and I couldn't hold it anymore."

Monae responds,

"I wish I knew why guys act like that. I was a ride or die for my son's Dad, I gave him all of me and all he did was lie and act stupid. Now all he does is call from jail, worried about if I'm talking to another guy. I'm so sick of him it's not funny. It's like every time I made up my mind that I was done with him I just had to let him back in. I can't keep doing that though, I'm not trying to struggle forever. Just making it by. That's why I'm working so hard now. I wanna buy a house and just not have to worry."

"Tell me about it." Reena replies.

After another sip of tea, she asks

"Where is your son at anyway?"

Monae tells her

"In Delaware with my sister. She said that she would watch him for me so I could go out. I'm about to go pick him up I'm a little bit. You wanna ride with me?"

"Yeah, I'll ride." Reena says.

~

After lamenting his abrupt misfortunes face down on his bed for over an hour, Lock finally lifts himself up like an almost broken prizefighter sneaking to his feet at the count of nine. The huge pile of ashes smoldering all around him was just yesterday a great life with a bright future. He has not even taken the time to rationalize everything that went on last night at the party, and now compounding the fracture, his hopes of courting Reena seem dashed, possibly forever. Lock was never infatuated with the streets or the drug game the way that Castle was. He hung out a little, but he was mainly accepted because of the family he came from. Lock could hang out on any block and not worry about being bothered. Just like everyone else in Salem, Lock has heard stories about Bad News, and he knows Attica's name, but he has no idea how easily death could have tapped him on the shoulder last night. The state of his company is promising but fragile. So many things need to go perfectly and there seems to be a wrench thrown into his cogs at every turn. He has to speak to Castle to figure out how to resolve the drama that threatens to smother his dreams. After showering, getting dressed and finally cleaning up the orange juice and pancakes fermenting on his floor, he will go to pay Castle a visit.

Lock brings his vehicle to a stop in front of Castle's house. After placing the car in park he finally musters the courage to send Reena a text. It simply reads "Can we talk?" He takes a quick second to check his Facebook, more so out of habit than actually caring what people are talking about at the moment. He doesn't even scroll through his timeline, he checks his notifications and then over to Instagram where he checks the pictures that he is tagged in from last night. A knock at his driver's side window breaks his concentration startling him enough to drop his phone in between his legs. It bounces off of the seat ultimately coming to rest on the car's floor slightly below the gas pedal. Before reaching to retrieve his device he rolls the window down for Mar Mar, he is six or seven years old and lives a few doors down from Castle. He asks Lock
"Hey Lock, you got a dollar?"

Relieved to see a smiling kid as opposed to an angry man, Lock reaches for his pocket faster than Doc Holliday could draw a pistol. He says, "Yo Mar Mar! Here boy, and don't knock on my window that hard again. And stay outta the street. Wait until I get out next time, OK?"

"OK, thanks!" he says with a huge snaggletooth grin.

Lock hits the one-touch up button which sends his window rolling to a close. He reaches down and grabs his phone before heading to Castle's door. He walks around the front of his car and into the sidewalk. As he approaches the steps which lead to the walkway before the door, Lock sees a shattered bottle of Hennessy and a Styrofoam

container of food spilled directly in front of the steps. He hops over the mess and up the walkway. He bangs on the door for 10 minutes before Castle finally answers.
"Damn man, what took you so long?" Lock asks.

Groggy and disheveled Castle replies
"I was sleep. I didn't get in til this morning."

"Man, you don't even wanna know about my morning. First off, I don't even know how I got home last night. The last thing I remember was the light coming on towards the end of the party. I don't remember leaving, and I definitely don't remember driving home." Lock says.

"You couldn't have been that drunk." Castle claims.

"I know, I definitely wasn't. I mean, I was feeling it a little, but not the type of drunk where I would forget everything, plus I'm not hungover too bad. I got a little headache, but I'm good."

He claps his hands together and continues by saying
"That's not the crazy part though. I wake up this morning with this jawn laying next to me!"

"Word!? Did you hit it!?" Castle asks excitedly.

Lock responds,
"Bro, I really don't know. I think so. She made it seem like we did, but I can't remember. We talked at the bar and kicked it back and forth, but how the hell did she end up in Salem?"

"That's crazy bro! What does she look like?" Castle asks.

Lock turns his head so that he is now looking at Castle from the corner of his eye and says,
"Amazing.."

He motions with his hand to give Castle an idea of her height.

"She's tall, super pretty, thick and everything. It gets worse though. So I wake up and I'm trying to figure out how this chick got in my bed, so I'm asking her questions and we're talking. My bedroom door flies open and it's Reena."

This opens up a touchy topic for Castle, he and Lock have not had a discussion about their mutual romantic enchantment for Reena that has seemingly managed to reach fever pitch simultaneously. He doesn't know for sure what happened after he left Reena's house that day and he managed to avoid speaking to either of them much in the ensuing days. He really does not want to ask about what happened next, but he feels like the arch of the conversation is forcing him to.

"So what happened?" he asks.

With a true hint of melancholy Lock states
"She stood there for a minute and didn't say anything. She just stared at me and I'm telling you, It woulda been better if she screamed and broke stuff."

Castle then asks
"So y'all started kicking it or something?"

"Not really." Lock replies.
Castle's phone vibrates and chimes while in his hand. He reads the newly delivered message which causes him to squint his eyes and press his lips together tightly after sucking his teeth with a small degree of contempt.

"What's up?" Lock asks as he looks to understand the cause of Castle's reaction.

"Nothing man, this chick next door just text me telling me to call her. I hate that shit. Why not just call me first, dummy?" Castle states.

"Oh, I thought it was something serious." Lock adds.

Castle says to him,
"I wonder what she wants though. I tried a couple times to get her to come through but she kept playing. I just gave up. She wants me to chase her or something and I ain't with all that."

"I feel you on that." Lock says.

Smiling, Castle says to Lock,

"Hold on for a second though, let me call and see what she's talking about. Might finally be my day!"

For the first time all day Lock gets a genuine laugh. Castle dials into his phone and places it to his ear. After a very brief phone call, he says to Lock,
"She's about to come here real quick. She said she gotta tell me something important."

"Don't look at me." Lock states.

Castle shrugs his shoulders as if he has no idea what she wants to talk about. Just then, there is a knock at the door prompting Castle to mildly walk over and open the portal. In walks Keema with her arms crossed tightly across her chest, she looks at the floor as she enters, not once making eye contact with Castle or Lock.

"Hey, what's up?" Castle asks.
He picks up on her nervousness and before she says anything in response he asks
"Everything OK?"

Still staring at the floor she says to him
"Look, I don't know what you got going on, but last night my boyfriend almost got shot out front because whoever it was thought that he was you."

"What!? What are you talking about?" Castle pleads.
"We left the diner and pulled up out front. I was driving and he was in the passenger seat. Then out of the corner of my eye I see something coming and I just froze. I couldn't move so I just fell next to my car. Whoever the guy was, ran around the other side and stood over top of my boyfriend with the gun pointed at him. He dropped all of our food, busted the bottle of liquor and everything. The only reason why I know that he was looking for you is 'cause he said your name. My boyfriend was on the ground and when he saw that it wasn't you, he just left. He wasn't trying to rob him 'cause he never checked his pockets or nothing. I screamed and told him that my boyfriend wasn't you. He didn't even run, he just put the gun away and walked off."

Both Castle and Lock are frozen still. Castle breathes in deeply while quickly blinking his eyes in erratic succession. He asks her,
"Did you see who it was?"

She glances up at Castle for a second, but then her eyes fall back to the floor, weighted by the trauma of a near-death experience.

"No, he had on all black. I didn't see nothing." she states.

Castle asks her,

"You couldn't see his face? Any tattoos on his hands or anything?"

"On his hands? Nigga all I know is that he had hands. I wasn't looking for no tattoos!" she states emphatically.

"Alright." Castle replies.

"I don't know about you, but I never saw a gun that close before. Especially with somebody about to use it. I didn't even go to sleep last night. I smoked a whole pack of cigarettes this morning and I don't even smoke. My boyfriend said he is never coming back to Salem. I didn't even wanna stay here last night but I was too scared to go back outside until the sun came up." Keema adds.

"Thanks, I appreciate you telling me." Castle says in a somber tone.

She skittishly wipes the left side of her face with her right hand in a downward motion as she says to Castle,

"I don't want my name to come up in this. Don't say you heard anything from me. I just had to let you know that somebody is out here trying to get you."

She walks to the door and before parting states,

"Remember, keep my name out of it, please. I got a son and I don't need nobody coming to my house trying to do something to me over stuff that I know nothing about."

"Nah, you're good." Castle replies and he shuts the door behind her and twists the deadbolt. Lock waits a few seconds for the coast to clear before completely losing his cool.

"What the fuck!?" he yells at the top of his lungs.

"We gotta figure out what's going on with this whole thing! What can we do to just straighten it all out? Like right now?!" Lock states.

"Real talk bro, I don't know. I tried to talk to Attica, but he ain't trying to hear it. That had to be Bad News last night. He snuck up on me once and I swear I never heard him until he was right there." Castle responds.

Lock paces the room as he says to Castle,
"I told you that street shit was gonna cause a problem. Why do I have to try to fix this now when it's all your fault? You don't even seem like you care!"

He flails his arms and speaks in a voice that mocks Castle's words as he says,
"Oh, nothing we can do. I guess that's the best you can come up with huh? I need a real answer! You could be dead right now bro! Dead! This is not a game. How many funerals we been to? Too many! Coulda been you next, then what? They're gonna come after me after that!?"

"We can't pay him. He wants too much. The only thing we can do is give him part of the company, or leave town maybe. We can just pack up and go to Atlanta. You can find us somewhere to stay down there, right?" Castle says.

Lock immediately shoots that idea down when he says,
"And then what? Never come back? Bro we have family here. My Grand Pop is here. I'm not running from these guys. Plus, what can we give him? He wants part of the company, but the company is nothing right now. It's just a bunch of promises floating around in the air. I'm trying to close the deal with Scott Campbell, but that's just talk right now, just like I'm trying to sign Stylez but that's nothing too. I don't have shit to give them! Set it up for me to talk to him and I'll just break it all down to him right there."

Castle responds
"I already tried to talk to them. I don't know bro, you know how to speak all proper and use big words so you might be able to hold Attica off for a while, but I doubt it. This dude talks crazy. He ain't even the one to worry about, it's really Bad News, but he only moves when Attica says so. I don't think you understand how serious this is. We may have to roll bro. It could get ugly and I know you ain't about this street life. Let's just chill though. I don't think they would try to do anything to you this fast, I'm the one that has to worry. It's all messed up right now."

Lock wears a face full of despair. At this moment he is defeated.

"I worked my whole life to try to build something and it's going to Hell right in front of my face. I don't do everything right, but I don't deserve this." he states.

His lament, like a mythical phoenix, undergoes a fiery transformation with the intensity aimed squarely at Castle. With two broad steps, the two men now stand face to face. Lock bites down on his teeth with great force while pushing words through his viced mouth and pointing his finger almost directly to the side of Castle's head as he says to him

"I should punch you in your face right now!"

Too close for comfort, Castle pushes Lock away and Lock reciprocates the action by shoving Castle as well. Both men fly back a few steps filling the room from floor to ceiling with tension and aggressive energy. Exasperated, Lock heads for the door, in a parting shot he says to Castle,

"You always make a mess and I gotta clean it up! Well what if I can't this time? Why is your stupidity ruining my life!? Not yours, mine!"

He twists the doorknob and pulls hard but the door doesn't budge. In his haste he fails to remember that Castle flipped the deadbolt. From the other side of the room Castle iterates,

"Man, shut your ass up. It's me that they're after and you're over here talking stupid."

Castle's words blow into Lock like a mighty gust of wind feeding the flickering flame in his belly and transforming it instantaneously into a wildfire. He charges at Castle with as much speed as he can generate inside the short distance. He lunges at Castle while throwing a lead right hand which only grazes the top of his head as he manages to duck at the last second. Momentum carries Lock into Castle while still in the air. He grips Lock around the waist and lifts him into the air. With nothing else to grab, Lock wraps his right arm around the back of Castle's neck and under his throat, making sure that as he flies to the ground Castle is along for the ride also. The two men tumble onto to the floor with Castle on top trying desperately to wrench his head free of Lock's desperate grip. Castle throws a few punches into Lock's midsection before blindly swinging in the area where he imagines is Lock's face. Lock squeezes tighter in an attempt to tire Castle by cutting off his air supply. Lock shimmies his hips and wraps his left leg around the back of Castle's right thigh. Feeling the extra pressure Castle uses both hands to create space between his windpipe and Lock's forearm. Lock feels his grasp slipping away and prepares himself to get to his feet as quickly as possible once Castle is loose. He decides to let go while simultaneously using the same right arm to thrust himself to the side and ultimately stand up before

Castle could launch an attack. Both tired and breathing heavily, the men don't say a word as Lock marches out of the house. They argued hundreds of times over the years, but this was the first time they fought since the playground in 1st grade.

Chapter 14

IT AIN'T HARD TO TELL

Across the street from East Side Projects, sitting a quarter mile or so from the road is an old brick building. Likely built before the turn of the Twentieth Century its functions have been many. However, to the recent generation and at least a few before, the claim on the property belongs to The Fraternal Order of The Elks. Salem residents refer to it as "The Elks Home" or even more simply "The Elks". Sitting behind the structure is a blacktopped basketball court with a goal at each end. In the 80's and 90's the games there were legendary. All of the best players in the area made the pilgrimage to the modest strip of asphalt with the giant reputation overcompensating for its lack of physical splendor.   Cars filled the parking lot and at times would line the court at its side, on the most festive of days music blared so loudly that the bounce of the ball would drown in the tide of high decibels. As time passed the days of "We're going there now" turned into talk of "You should have been there when" and though the hoops still stood, any balls passing through the iron cylinders, having been heaved with perfect trajectory, were done so to little or no fanfare. The glory days had faded away, just like the once freshly painted lines on the court. By the time Schemer was a kid, The Elks was all but the last resort. The edges of the court had begun to chip and crumble, and one of the backboards bore evidence of target practice. Kids still found their way to the court from time to time, Schemer being one of those who would occasionally make a trip. He loved basketball-it was one of the things that allowed him to truly be a kid with no worries. South Jersey in the early 2000's was in the midst of a revolution, as evidenced by the attire of every young boy who called the area home. Number 3 Philadelphia 76ers jerseys and cornrowed heads wrapped in folded bandanas stretched as far as the eye could see. For Schemer and all of his friends, wearing the name Iverson in between their shoulder blades was more important than drinking water or eating food. Even kids who rooted for other teams loved Bubba Chuck like he was their brother or best friend. To not be able to pledge undying devotion to the army of "The Answer" by dressing in the upper half of his uniform while trying to perfect a crossover before hoisting up prayers or charging to the rack with reckless abandon was a fate worse than that of a leper. Schemer was lucky enough to have two jerseys, one blue and the other black. He wore them every chance he got and almost never set foot on a court without donning the battle armor of the biggest heart the game had ever seen.

Just like in everyday life, Schemer was cerebral as a basketball player. He was smaller than most kids his age yet often took to the court with kids older than he. Quickness was an attribute, but he would try to pick up on the tendencies of the other player and exploit any weaknesses he could find to compensate his vertical inadequacy. He took no more than each situation was willing to offer in hopes that an accumulation of small wins would lead to an overall victory on the court. There was one particular day that in the manner of basketball games was not much different from any other. Some of his shots fell perfect while others hit the iron harder than a forging hammer. For the most part, his jump shot was working and his first step felt a little more fluid, being as though he was superstitious like many players tend to be, he felt that maybe his new "Hold My Own" tattoo had something to do with the extra burst. Actually, the tattoo was not real, his friend Jeremy drew on Schemer's right shoulder with a sharpie, but it made him feel a little more like Iverson that day.

After several games of two-on-two, Jeremy decided that he was done for the day which in essence ended activities for the other three as well. The only other option the remaining players had was to play Monster. A form of basketball played in many different areas and regions, where each player fends for himself in efforts to be the first to score twenty one points. A scored bucket gives the player three attempted free throws on a make it and get another shot basis. The free throws are taken from the three-point line and if a player has accumulated twenty points and misses the game-winning free throw, their score reduces to twelve and the game continues. This is usually a game that is played to start the day, not to finish it, so when Jeremy quit it took the air out of the other guys and it was time to leave. The boys gathered their things and started off on their journey to the street, which was a bit of a hike in itself. As they approached the building, one of the older kids named AJ thought it would be a good idea to break in.

"For what?" Jeremy asked.

"Man, they have food and stuff in there. It might even be some money in the cash register." AJ stated.

"Why would they leave money in the register? That's stupid" Schemer inserted.

In an attempt to convince the bunch to help with his ploy, AJ said to them,
"Stop acting like punks. They got a whole bunch of liquor in there too. You know they got a bar in there. It's probably mad boxes of chips and everything."

Jeremy then asked,
"Well how are we gonna get in?"

AJ replied,
"The handle on the inside of the door is one of those bars that you just push to open. It don't latch all the way, so if one of us kicks the door hard it'll pop open a couple of inches, then somebody just has to be standing there to catch it before it shuts again."

"How do you know that?" Jeremy asked.

"Cause I went in there before. Not too long ago they gave us a few bags of chips and a soda cause we helped carry stuff in." AJ replied.

Schemer then says,
"Yeah, I was there. They did let us help. I don't know if you saw it, but they got an alarm in there too."

"Man, you know how long it'll take them to get here? We can just run in and out and be gone."

Schemer was younger but much more of a technical thinker. He said to AJ,
"It's not about that. It's a long way to the street from here. Even if we make it all the way, by the time we get there the cops will probably be pulling up or close enough to see us. Even if we go across the field on the other side, it's wide open and they'll be able to see us that way too. Plus it ain't even dark yet."

AJ completely ignored Schemer's reasoning and said,

"Stop being scared."

To be labeled as scared or soft was a badge of nearly the highest dishonor and Schemer took it personally.

"I ain't scared but I ain't trying to get caught either." he replied.

"Well you stay out here and be the lookout. Vince, once we get in here go straight to the kitchen and see what you can find, and Jeremy, hit the bar and grab as many bottles as you can." AJ said to the boys.

The back door entrance was fixed with an incline as opposed to steps and was cased in by a metal handrail. This meant that there was no way to get a running start in order to kick the door hard enough for it to pop open. AJ stood with his back to the door, clinching the handrail tightly with both hands. He generated all of the force that he could find and sent his foot smashing into the door with a massive back kick. The impact was thunderous and echoed out over the empty area. Sound being no indicator of success, the door barely opened at all. AJ got back into his stance and gripped the rails even harder. He clenched his teeth and focused on sending every bit of energy available to his right leg. As he began his kick he used his arms to thrust himself off of the railing into the direction of the threshold. His foot met the door earlier than before unleashing a much more damaging strike. Jeremy was able to stick his palm inside the door as it snapped open a few inches and in a flash the three boys disappeared into the building. Schemer thought that it was a terrible idea but his loyalty would not allow him to leave them there. His heart raced and his stomach was jittery as he paced around anxiously. Each time he turned to pace back he would lightly kick the ground twice with the toe of each of his sneakers. Seconds could not burn away fast enough as the other boys remained inside for what seemed like forever. The area was completely silent, so when Schemer heard an engine and the sound that small rocks or gravel makes under car tires he turned as white as a ghost. He peeked around the building but only slightly as he did not want to be seen. His vision was completely impaired by the headlights beaming directly in his direction. He quickly had astutely remembered a technique that his uncle used to distinguish police cars as they approached on the street. He glanced around the building for a second look, this time squinting one eye and holding his hand flattened vertically just below his eyes. This blocks the light enough to distinguish whether or not the approaching vehicle adorns lights on top of the hood. Sure enough, not only was the car edging nearer a police cruiser, but it had drawn a lot closer due to Schemer needing a second shot before making the proper identification. He stumbled into a full stride around the railing and up the ramp. He snatched at the door's handle only to be met with denial. He could not get in to warn the others of the converging threat. He pounded at the dense metal door with the base of his closed fist before turning and sending a few swift kicks with the sole of his foot. He cupped his mouth with his hands and yelled to his faction,

"Cops, cops, Cops! Hurry up"

He dashed around to the far side of the building opposite of the direction from which the squad car approached. Seconds later AJ blasted through the door arms filled with potato chips, cookies and crackers. Jeremy and Vince were not far behind hoarding a bevy of snacks and alcohol. Before Jeremy fully breached the exit the police were in position and exiting the car. One of the officers yelled,

"Stop! Police!"

None of the four boys complied as they made their way through the open field. The officers gave chase and Jeremy was apprehended almost immediately, followed by Vince not long after. Sirens then started to sound out closely as well as faintly in the distance. Schemer, who was the first to flee had a bit of a head start and managed to make it over the fence and into the backyard of a house on Keasby Street. The first responding officers never saw his face only getting a glimpse of his white shorts, Allen Iverson jersey and red wave cap. He tripped, rolled and jumped back to his feet in a full stride as he hustled through the yard and onto the street. He flew across Keasby and into the projects, breathing heavily but too scared to completely stop, his one hundred meter dash style of running had slowed to the sluggish jog of a tired marathoner. Once across the parking lot and behind the buildings on the other side, Schemer crouched by a group of bushes with his back against a fence and tried desperately to catch his breath. Sirens sounded in what seemed like every direction. He lived so far away and though it did not matter at the moment, he knew that he would later be furious for leaving his basketball behind. As AJ reached the street, he was apprehended by officers responding as backup. Schemer was the only remaining fugitive as he sat hunched in a dark corner in the rear of the projects. He swiped his read wave cap from his head and balled it up, placing it into the left pocket of his basketball shorts. He took off his jersey, rolled it up and threw it over his shoulder. Now wearing white shorts and a white t-shirt, he took a few seconds to calm himself before heading through a hole cut in the fence nearby and down a project shortcut that would lead him closer to safety. Each step brought Schemer closer to the refuge of home, but it felt to him like a journey of a thousand miles. He spent all of his brain power trying not to look guilty as he strolled down the street, butterflies flapped inside of him with every approaching vehicle. After finally turning the last corner before home, he heard a squeak. He had heard the sound before and there was no way for him to confuse it with anything else. He ignored it and kept walking. That second a

police car pulls over just in front of him toward the curb on a sharp angle while also facing the wrong direction in the road. Schemer is trying his best to remain calm, as he knew that often times just appearing to be uptight or nervous will cause an officer to get out of his car and begin to ask questions. With his head facing down, Schemer remained cool until he heard a voice call out,
"Hey, let me talk to you for a second."

He looks up wearing a contrived mask of astonishment and asked
"Who me?"

The officer responded saying,
"Yeah, come here."

For the first time, Schemer broke his stride. He thought about his odds of getting away if he ran, but when he glanced over his shoulder it became apparent that running was not an option as two more officers approached from the rear. Feeling trapped, he walked over to the officer and said,
"Yeah?"

The officer asked,
"Where are you headed?"

"Home, I live right up that way." Schemer replies.

"Where are you coming from?" the officer asked.

"I'm coming from my friend's house." Schemer said.

The officer asked him,
"Where does your friend live at?"

"Around the corner, why?" Schemer responded.
The officer then said,
"So you weren't just over at the basketball court a little while ago?"

"Nope. What court?" Schemer asked.

"Don't play stupid with me you little punk!" The officer said in a much more fiery tone.

He grabbed Schemer by the arm and said to him,

"Why don't you have this jersey on huh? Why is it on your shoulder and not on?" He throws Schemer against the rear quarter panel of the squad car and asks him "What's in your pockets?"

Schemer yells back at him "I ain't got nothing."

As he begins to rummage through Schemer's shorts he said "You don't have anything that can stick me do you? Any knives, weapons or hypodermic needles."

"Man, I said I ain't got nothing." Schemer replied.

He pulls out of Schemer's left pocket the balled up durag. He then grabs Schemer's left hand and places it behind his back as he simultaneously kicked his left foot in an effort to spread Schemer's legs. He cuffed his left wrist and then his right. He placed Schemer in the back seat of the car and said to him "Hang tight for a minute, OK?"

He then went over to speak with the other 3 officers at the scene and with the red wave cap acting as the evidence that they felt they needed, they took Schemer to the station and charged him along with the other boys with breaking and entering, theft, resisting arrest and a host of other charges. Many of the charges were reduced or dropped and the members of The Elks Lodge refused to press charges. Schemer still had to complete community service which was nothing compared to the beating that his Dad laid on him. It was then that Schemer understood that he would never let his loyalty lead him to ruin.

***

With a mind never truly at rest, Schemer did not get much sleep after Attica sent News to kill Castle. He felt like it was a bad choice, and after finally catching a few winks and waking to start his day, he still feels that it is an egregious error. The first thing that he does is grab his phone to comb through social media for the wave of "rest in peace" and "stop the violence" posts that saturate his timeline whenever someone is killed inside the city. Devoid of any such cries of foul play, he closes the apps and calls Attica. Neither men ever discuss matters in detail over the phone so when Schemer asks

"What's it looking like?"

Attica replies,
"Nothing much. They threw a little get-together but not a lot of people showed up."

This is Attica's way of telling Schemer that the plan was in place and the target never arrived.

"Where are you?" Schemer asks.

Attica replies,
"I'm about to shoot to News' crib. Meet me over there."

Before ending the call Schemer says to him,
"Word, I'll check you out when I get there."

After hanging up the phone he sits there for a moment, completely still. He closes his eyes to focus more deeply as he tries to come up with the best way to convince Attica to call off his hit on Castle. He knows it will not be easy but it is much less difficult to stop a speeding locomotive than it is to put one back together after crashing into a brick wall with a full head of steam.

Schemer arrives to find News and Attica eating breakfast food without him.
"What's that, bacon?" he asks.

"You know damn well I don't play those games. No pork on my fork." Attica replies.

"I'm just messing with you. How y'all gonna get food without me though?" Schemer asks.
"It's some home fries and eggs leftover in there. You can have it if you want it." News states.

"Gee thanks. I see how it is. Niggas just forget about me huh? It's cool, I'm gonna remember it though. One of y'all is gonna be hungry one day." Schemer says.

Schemer goes into the kitchen and retrieves the white styrofoam tray containing the extra food. He opens the lid and begins to break the crunchy top shell of the home fires with a plastic fork. He sprinkles in some salt and pepper before adding ketchup to the potatoes and reconvening with Attica and News in the main room. Once there he begins to ask questions in between huge bites of food.
"So what happened last night?" he asks.

"Nothing. I stayed out there damn near all night and he never showed up." News responds.

Schemer shovels around in his eggs with his eyes locked inside the tray and states "Well maybe that was a sign. I think we should just chill on that for a second."

"Don't start talking that stupid shit again." Attica says.

"It's not stupid, it's just better for business." Schemer replies.

"You ain't even in charge of the business. Let me handle that." Attica snaps.

Schemer replies,
"So what does that have to do with it being a good idea or a bad idea?"

"Who are you talking to?" Attica barks.

"I'm just saying." Schemer quickly suggests.

Attica, clearly agitated says to Schemer,
"I don't give a shit about what you're saying. I already told you. It's happening. End of story. The nigga gotta go."

Never one to see a door as totally closed, Schemer responds with
"But like I said, nobody knows that he owes you money, and his friend, what's the other boy's name? He's a square. The only reason he bucked up a little bit the other night is because he don't know how real it can get. I'm sure Castle probably schooled him by now. I'm just trying to see us all come out on top. News, you even said that

catching too many bodies back to back is gonna bring the Feds. How can we make money after that? You're willing to throw everything away over a soft little dude and his college friend? That's stupid bro!"

"I ain't never been stupid, and I'll show you stupid if you think I'm bullshitting. I don't have time for all your tricks and head games. Sometimes you just gotta show niggas what time it is." Attica says to him.

Schemer replies,
"But.."

Attica interrupts him almost immediately and says to him,
"No buts. It's over. I'm not talking about this shit no more."

"I was gonna say that if he was willing to pay you some money, you should at least get that. Don't kill him for free when he was willing to pay five or ten bands." Schemer suggests.

"Now that's a good idea. Set it up for tonight. Tell Castle that News is gonna meet him to pick up the bread and that if he pays up then everything is good. Make sure you call him from a prepaid phone so that when they go through his last calls it won't come back to none of us." Attica orders.

"Cool, I got you. I'll try to hit him now." Schemer adds.

He gets up from his seat and walks to the door.
Attica leans closer to News and says in a very low voice
"I want you to keep an eye on him."

"What do you mean?" News asks.

"I don't know. I can't tell if this dude is still down for the cause. Make sure he don't try to pull some sneaky shit one day. If so, I hate to say it but he gotta go."
"Word. Say no more." News responds.

Later that night around 11 PM News arrives at the corner of Eakin and Wesley to meet Castle. His black on black New Jersey Devils hat is turned to the back and his hoodie is drawn right around his neck with the strings tied into a bow. A car approaches and he walks off as to mask any suspicion that may be raised if he were to stand there. Once the car makes its turn, he reversed direction and heads back to the meeting spot. After a minute, Castle eases around the corner visibly uneasy.

"What's up? You got it?" News asks.

"Yeah, everything is good." Castle replies.

"Well pass off, I ain't trying to be out here all night" News claims.

"I just wanna make sure that after this we're good. Attica is gonna leave us alone and I don't owe him shit after this." Castle says.

News responds with a quick
"Yeah."

" No man, I need to hear you say it." Castle begs.

"Yeah you're good, now give me the bread before I smack the shit out of you." News barks.

"Alright man, here." Castle says.
He reaches into his back pocket and pulls out a wrinkled envelope that appears stuffed. As he lifts his arm to hand it over to News a minivan flies up and screeches to a halt. Out jump four large men in tactical gear. The front of their bulletproof vests read "Police" and they order both men to the ground with guns drawn. Before Castle and News were face down on the concrete three additional cars pull up and an entire SWAT team canvases the scene like a school of hungry piranhas.

"Where's the drugs?" one of them asks as he places all of his weight into the center of Castle's back with a knee.

"I don't know what you're talking about" Castle manages to force out under the heavy pressure of the officer's body weight.

"I know it's somewhere. The longer I have to look the worse it's gonna be for you." the officer says.

As one officer keeps his knee squarely spiked into Castle's back, two others empty his pockets while he is being cuffed.

"You don't have anything to stick me on you right? No needles, no nothing?" they ask.

"Man, what I need a needle for?" Castle replies.

Bad News is undergoing the same fate. The piranhas taste blood when one of them yells out.

"Jackpot! This one has a weapon."

They lift News to his feet by his arms and walk him over to the car where he is placed into the backseat. They eject the clip from News' gun and place it on the hood of the patrol car. Castle is now lifted to his feet as well and the officers begin to drill into him.

"Tell me where the drugs are now and I'll take it easy on you. The longer I have to look, the longer I'm gonna kick your ass once I find it. Do yourself a favor you little fake ass Tupac."

"I don't know how many times I gotta tell you, I don't got no drugs. We was just talking. We didn't even do nothing wrong." Castle pleads.

After a few minutes of back and forth, Castle is placed into a separate car and both men are driven to the police station. Once inside they are handcuffed to a bench near the back of the building where they await processing. Castle's wrist is cuffed way too tight and he is starting to lose feeling to the outer side of his pinky finger. Bound next to him, News sits calmly. He asks Castle.

"You set me up?"

Castle immediately replies

"Hell no man. Why would I do that? For all of that, I woulda never showed up."

News looks him directly in the eye and says

"I hope not, but if I find out you did. Then I might as well be talking to myself because I'm sitting next to a dead man.

Chapter 15

FRIEND OR FOE

October 14, 1987 was a normal Wednesday in Salem. The sun fought through a slight overcast and the temperature hovered around 43 degrees Fahrenheit. Not windy by any account; however, the changing leaves already rusted had begun to fall and tumble along the sides of the roadways. Halloween decorations were well underway and peppered neighborhood houses with jack o' lanterns, vampires and witches. Unremarkable happenings on a day that started out like any other autumn Wednesday in Salem, but news would soon ride into town like a lightning bolt and completely electrify the city! Charles J. Pedersen, who called Salem home nearly his entire life was being awarded The Nobel Prize in Chemistry. He worked at nearby DuPont for over forty years, and during that time managed to write two studies that were considered classics inside the science community well before Stockholm came calling. Pedersen's work gave way to over 65 patents, but it was his study of crown ethers-a term in which he coined-that would result in his being crowned a Nobel Laureate.

As an energetic elementary school kid, Castle, like most kids his age loved to watch cartoons. One of his favorite animated tales was Dexter's Laboratory. Castle would glue himself in front of the television whenever his most loved show aired. He even pretended that Mandark (Dexter's arch nemesis) lived next door, which was the case in the show. He also begged his Mom to have another baby and insisted that she be named Dee Dee just like Dexter's sister. When he was in the 4th grade his classroom took part in a career day. As the teacher went from student to student giving them the opportunity to rise and voice their future goals to the class, the routine responses jumped from the mouths of the prepubescent hopefuls. There were dreams of becoming doctors, lawyers and even The President Of The United States. When Castle's turn was called he stood to his feet nervously and debated about whether or not he should just pretend to what to be a doctor so that he could quickly return to his seat. Castle did not want to be a doctor, he wanted to be like Dexter. As he quickly finalized his decision he blurted out

"I want to be a scientist."

His teacher responded

"That's a great career! Why do you want to be a scientist Donovan?"

"I want to be a genius, and I want to have my own laboratory and invent stuff!" Castle said enthusiastically.

As an act of encouragement, his teacher told him

"There was a famous scientist from right here in Salem. You may not understand how big of a deal it is, but he won The Nobel Prize a few years before you kids were born. That is a really big honor. I think there is a book that talks about him in the library. The next time we go down you should ask about it."

Castle's face was powerless to hide his excitement. True to his teacher's words, the magnitude of a Nobel Prize winner being from his town would not fully sink in for several years. The only barometer Castle had for the magnitude was that every February during Black History Month, one of the three things that they were taught religiously was about Martin Luther King Jr., his "I Have A Dream" speech or that he had won The Nobel Peace Prize. Castle felt that if Charles Pedersen won the same award as Martin Luther King Jr. then he must be famous.

The next week when it was time for Castle's class to have their library session, he rushed to be the first in line and asked for the book on the man with whom his fascination had grown like the flicker of an ill-disposed of match falling into dry California grass. He took the book home and he read it over and over. Some of the words were so big that he had to find other books just to get the meanings, but that didn't stop Castle-he was hooked. Somehow Castle acquired information that Pedersen lived in a house on Chestnut Street, so after school on Friday he walked through that street even though it was the opposite direction from where he lived. His voyage turned up nothing and he headed home. He dropped off his books and grabbed his bike, intent on a second trip to Chestnut. Once there, he slowed his bike as he approached the house but did not come to a complete stop. He let his bike coast three houses down and then turned around for another pass. He repeated this routine for two hours, hoping to get a glimpse of Mr. Pedersen. Eventually, he grew tired and was also terribly hungry so he set out for home having not completed his mission. The next day he returned early, but again was unable to cross paths with his new hero. On Sunday he returned and his lack of success that day compounded by his previous fails began to take a toll on his morale. He made up his mind that Monday would be his day. After school let out he marched over to Chestnut Street with the book in his hand. He recited in his head what he would say to Mr. Pedersen when they met. He wondered if Mr. Pedersen would be nice to him and if he had a laboratory in his basement just like Dexter. He imagines it full of beakers, Bunsen burners and laboratory flasks. Crystal clear in his imagination were the tubes crisscrossing the room from different machines where Mr. Pedersen must have stood at a cluttered table mixing potions like Dexter.

Maybe he could learn to mix a few himself. As he approached the house, his anxiousness spread from his core to the tips of his fingers. His first pass of the dwelling was done without a hitch in his step. He turned to walk past again, this time stopping directly in front of the house. He looked up at the front door and contemplated going up to knock on it. Fear quickly took over and he took a few steps in continuance of his pattern of patrolling back and forth but stopped in his tracks. He fought with himself right there on the sidewalk, struggling intently to draw up the courage to knock or ring the doorbell. So preoccupied with his inner struggle, he never noticed the tall thin man approach him.

"Hey kid, you alright?" he asked.

Castle snapped out of the trance that he had fallen into and his eyes shot upward to look at the man who stood at his side. He was wearing a tan jacket and blue jeans with a checkered button-up shirt. After quickly gathering his wits, Castle replied in the most timid voice imaginable

"Does Mr. Pedersen live in this house here?" as he pointed up at the Victorian structure.

"Who?" asked the tall man.

Castle produced the book that he had been holding tightly in his grasp and flipped to the page where there was a picture of Mr. Pedersen. He showed the picture to the man as he stated,

"You know, Charles Pedersen? The Nobel Prize winner. He's a scientist."

In a eureka moment the man says in a drawn-out fashion,

"Oh!"

He then wrinkles his brow and takes quick but deep inhale and exhale before saying

"Yeah kid, I'm sorry but he used to live there. He died some years back. I think it was '89 or '90." Castle was floored. His teacher never mentioned that Mr. Pedersen died just two years after receiving his Nobel Prize and years before Castle was even born. The book from the library was printed in 1988 and at that time Mr. Pedersen was still alive. Having his dreams dashed in such a manner caused Castle to never look at science the same. He still loved Dexter, but the magic that had been building inside of his imagination would never be the same.

***

"Castle!" yelled the approaching officer.

"Up on your feet." he states as he reaches to uncuff Castle from the bench in which he has been constrained to for the last three hours. The key twists and the bracelet eases its iron bear hug from Castle's wrist, the feeling of pins and needles still suffocating his fingers as he tries to rub away the indentations caused by the metal ligature. He is walked into the same room that News has been led to about an hour earlier. The electronic fingerprinting machine acts almost as a novelty as immediately after his hands are painting for the manual process. The roller dispersing ink over his fingers and palms is hard and the ink is cold. One by one his fingers are rolled from right to left, documenting the uniqueness of his touch. After several attempts at scrubbing the soil away with a small dirty bar of soap and cold water, Castle's hands still bare evidence of the arrest ritual as tiny faded blotches remain to tell the tale. Castle is then guided into another room where two desks sit parallel to each other and are covered in paperwork. The walls are flooded with wanted posters and bulletins. There is a filing cabinet in the corner and a wooden coat rack stands at attention to its side. Castle is told to have a seat in the wooden chair facing the desk near the back of the room. As he sits, the chair creaks and the legs make an awkward noise pattern as he pulls the chair closer.

"So Donovan, I was wondering if you could help me out?" asked the detective.

"Help you out?" Castle asked in a puzzled manner.

While twirling a pen around between the pointer and middle fingers of both hands, the detective states,

"I need you to tell me where the drugs are. Now if you play ball, I can take that into consideration and talk to some people-we'll go easy on you. If you don't help me out, there's nothing I can do."

"What drugs are you talking about? I don't know nothing about no drugs." Castle replies.

"Listen, we already know everything. We know that you were there to score some cocaine, and I just need you to tell me where you hid it at. You help me and I help you, or else you're gonna end up like your friend there. He's on his way out to the county jail right now and I can send you right behind him." the detective said to Castle.

"For what? I didn't do nothing. And I don't know nothing about no drugs." Castle responds emphatically.

"Look, I don't care if it was yours or his. For all I know it was his, but when we find it and nobody claims it you're both gonna wear it. Now if you're the first one to speak up, then maybe it just belongs to him. I'm not telling you to say that, but maybe that's the case." he says to Castle.

He looks at the detective and says to him,
"I don't know what to tell you. I don't know about no drugs at all. I was just out there minding my business and having a conversation and y'all hopped out all crazy. Why am I still even here? Am I charged with something? Take me to jail or let me go."

Frustrated with Castle's lack of cooperation, the detective stands to his feet and pounds the desk while saying,
"You're a little punk. You think you're cool but you're a punk and I'm gonna bust your ass. You think we don't know what you do? We see everything. You're on my radar now so it's only a matter of time. I tried to help you but since you don't want my help, you're on your own. Watch yourself out there because I'm definitely watching you!"

"Can I go now?" Castle asks.

"In a second." the detective replies.

He leaves the room and returns less than a minute later handing Castle a green sheet of paper. Castle begins to read it and cries out,
"Disorderly person?! How are you gonna charge me with being disorderly when I ain't do nothing? I was standing there chilling and y'all came and bothered me. Whatever man."

Castle gets up and heads to the door. After exiting the room he must wait to be buzzed out into the vestibule before then exiting out to freedom. He stands there smoldering mad yet containing his fury as much as possible. He doesn't want the detective to know how upset he is so he smiles as he waits for the electronic lock to release. Suddenly he heard a buzz followed by a clicking sound. He pushes the door and breezes through that and another before ultimately setting foot on Broadway with a green sheet in his hand and a detective's threats echoing in his head. It's way too late for him to call for a ride so he walks to retrieve his car before finally making it home. His night is somewhat restless as he recounts the words of not only the detective, but Bad News as well. Life in the drug game is always dangerous and uncertain. As of late, though, his life is more like a minefield. One false step or miscalculation and he will be stretched out at Evergreen Cemetery amongst his grandparents and many others from the city whose numbers were called. As fear and self-doubt creep in, he wonders if he can handle the pressure. The same boiling water that softens a potato also hardens an egg. His reaction to this recent adversity will most likely determine whether he lives or dies.

Castle awakes to a full day ahead of him. As he had done many days before when he would rush outside to catch early morning customers, he brushes his teeth, washes his face and puts on the same clothes he had on last night. He grabs his phone to make a call before going into the kitchen to put the finishing touches on a bottle of Sprite in the refrigerator. It takes quite a few rings before his call is answered, and after a quick gulp of soda Castle says
"Yo, what's up?"
He paces over to the table and sits while the person in the other end of the phone speaks. After listening intently he says
"Meet me in Swedesboro. It's pretty quiet out there."
He gets up from the table and picks up his car keys, bringing an end to the brief conversation by stating
"Yeah, I'm on my way out the door right now. OK, see you there."
Swedesboro is a short twenty-minute ride from Salem but it is much quieter and nothing goes on there. A good place to not be seen by anyone from the city. Castle pulls into the CVS drugstore and parks. Having not eaten anything he goes in to get a few snacks while he waits. He buys a bag of chips, an almond Hershey bar, a Kit Kat and a bottle of soda. After paying for his candy and drink he sits in his car listening to music while he waits. The song "Blue Laces" is playing and in the third verse, Nipsey Hussle recalls a gun battle where his friend gets shot and he has to drive him to the hospital. As the words flow from the speakers and into Castle's ear, they send him into a daydream as puts himself in the shoes of the orator and imagines himself shooting his way out of a tough situation. He then looks down at his phone before a car pulls up next to him on the passenger side. Opening Castle's door and dropping down to have a seat next to him is Schemer.

"What's up?" Schemer asks.

Castle replies,
"You tell me."
The conversation is cordial but not completely comfortable.
"How'd the meeting go?" Schemer asks.

"Nigga, the task force hopped out on us and took us both downtown. They kept me for a minute but let me go after a while. They bagged News with a burner though. I don't know if he had anything else." Castle replies.

"You left the money home like I told you, right?" Schemer asks.

Castle replies to him,
"Yeah man. Why'd you tell me to do that anyway? What's going on with this whole thing? You call me once and tell me to meet him with the bread. Then you call me back and say don't bring the bread, but bring an envelope full of McDonald's coupons. What the hell was that for?"

Schemer lets a deep exhale pass through his slightly opened lips and he tells Castle
"To keep it all real, News was there to clip you. I couldn't tell you that because I thought you might get scared and wouldn't show up even. I knew that if you didn't show up it would be worse for you. I put a plan in place to save your life basically."

"So you called the cops?" Castle asks.
"I wouldn't look at it like that. I just have them a fake tip about a drug deal going down." Schemer responds.

"How did you know they'd show up?" Castle asks Schemer.

"When won't they show up for a easy bust?" Schemer insists.

He then turns his shoulders more squarely toward Castle and says to him
"Look I'm the only friend you got out here. Attica is gunning for you and News don't care, he'll just do whatever Attica wanna do. I need you to lay low for a couple of days until I figure everything out. Don't tell anybody about anything that I told you."

"Why are you helping me?" Castle asks.

"I didn't wanna see you die over some dumb shit. I know you don't deserve that." Schemer replies.

"I don't know what made you look me out, but thanks." Castle states.

Schemer then tells him,
"I'm probably gonna need you to introduce me to your partner too. I gotta have both of y'all in the fold to be able to bring this thing to a happy ending."

"Yeah well ain't no happy ending with us right now. You're gonna have to talk to him yourself." Castle adds.

"OK, I'll get up with him at some point but it's not that important right this moment. Just stay under the radar for a while. It may be a few weeks, let's wait and see if they give News a bail or not. Attica has heart, but he ain't a shooter like News, so you should be safe for the most part. He's hot-headed though so he may try to hire somebody else or have one the young boys try to get at you. Just keep your mouth shut about everything and if you're not sure then call my phone." Schemer instructs.

He gives Castle a handshake and exits the carriage before getting into his car and pulling away. Schemer's plans are never one-sided, so in crippling Attica's efforts, which he deems necessary, he was also able to endear himself to Castle by making him believe that his actions had been born of kindness. Happy to be alive and at least able to breathe with News behind bars, Castle doesn't question the root cause nearly as critically as he should.

Later in the evening Castle sends Reena a text telling her that he is going to be stopping by. He arrives just as she finishes studying for an exam later in the week. She answers the door wearing a purple sweatsuit with colorful socks one nothing like the other.

"Damn girl, you look like the crazy lady." Castle jokes.

"Whatever, I'm comfortable." Reena says to him.

"I know I'm just kinda popping up on you, my fault for being kinda distant for a minute. I just didn't know how to handle that whole situation. I do wanna talk to you though." Castle states.

Reena replies,
"Yeah, a lot was going on that night. What do you want to talk about though?"

Castle melts into his seat and says to her
"Everything. I just don't know what to do about anything right now and you're the only person that I can talk to."

"I understand. You don't feel like you can talk to Lock? Not that I'm saying that you can't talk to me because you can, but I know that you usually tell him everything." Reena says.

"Nah, that's part of it. So much is going on with the company, I don't even know if we are still gonna have a company to tell the truth. We got into a real fight yesterday." Castle tells her.

"Like a real bad argument?" she asks.

Castle responds,
"Nah, we came to blows."

"What?! Why?" Reena asks.

"Long story, I'll tell you all about it. Maybe you should try to talk some sense into him though." Castle says.

"I don't really have anything to say to Lock. I'm sorry, but you're gonna have to fix that on your own." Reena states firmly.

Castle wipes his hand down his face and says to her
"I'll figure something out. But what are you doing Friday? I need to get out and just chill. You wanna go to the movies with me? Maybe go get something to eat too?"

"I don't know. I'm not in the mood for going out. Plus, I know we have some stuff going on between us that we never talked about and then you kinda disappeared so it's just kinda sitting out there. So much has happened in the past few days and I don't want to give you the wrong impression." she says.

"Well, I felt whatever it was that you're talking about, but I just left because I didn't want to try to take it there and compete with Lock, but you know how I feel. It's no secret that I like you. Right now I'm just asking you to hang out with me though. Real talk." Castle pleads.

"OK, I can do that. What do you wanna go see? And you know I'm greedy so you're definitely taking me to get something to eat too." Reena says to him.

"I don't know what's coming out this weekend, but I'll look it up." Castle replies. He pulls out his phone, tapping the screen a few times before saying,
"Did you eat yet? You want some pizza? I was thinking about going to Pat's."

"I don't want pizza but you can get me a order of chicken fingers and fries." she replies.

"OK-call it in. I'll go get it and I'll be right back." he states.

Reena sits on the couch and turns on the television. She picks up her phone to check Snapchat and sees a text from Lock that reads "I wanna talk to you. Stop playing, you know I love you." She does not respond.

As Friday rolls around, Castle is in a much better frame of mind. His problems still linger in the back of his mind but most times he is able to tune out the bad thoughts. He has taken Schemer's advice and has stayed largely out of public view. He and Reena have considered themselves friends since childhood, but this last week has been different than any other in their lives. He drives to her house at 7:30 PM and sends her a text that reads "I'm out front." She promptly replies "Rude! Come to the door." He exits and walks to her door giving it three sharp knocks with the knuckle of his middle finger. Reena answers and says to him
"Boy, don't ever text a girl and tell her you're out front. You walk up to the door to greet her. Don't you know anything?"

"My bad." Castle responds.

Once inside the car Reena notices that in the cup holder sits her favorite drink-a Starbucks mocha frappuccino.
"Is this mine?" she asks.

"Yeah, that's for you." Castle replies.

"Aww, you're so sweet. This still doesn't make up for that text, but it's a start." Reena states jokingly

Castles car is freshly detailed. The dashboard is shining, the carpet is immaculate and the wonderful smell is like a walk through Versailles. Castle is wearing a red hoodie with a gold Basquiat crown designed on the front.

"I really like that shirt." Reena says to Castle.

"Really? I just got this. Somebody made it for me. Stop acting like you know about Basquiat." Castle says with a laugh.

"Who?" Reena replies.

"Jean-Michel Basquiat. He was an artist, and he always drew this crown." Castle tells her as they ride to their destination.

"Oh, I have no idea, I just really like the shirt." Reena says.

Castle explains
"To keep it real, I didn't know who he was until I kept hearing Jay Z say his name. After that, I looked it up and he was pretty dope."

"I'll look him up when I get a chance." she says.

After drinking some of her frappuccino she says to Castle,
"This is the most we've hung out probably ever. I can't think of a time when we hung out for five days straight. It's like I knew as soon as I got gone that you were gonna be coming by."

She laughs and continues to say,
"It was fun though, I really enjoyed hanging out with you this week. It took my mind off of a lot of drama, and you helped me catch up on all of my shows. I feel like I accomplished something this week."

"So you ain't gonna give me credit for helping you study?" Castle asks.

"Oh yeah, definitely that too. You were a big help." she says.

"You had to take that this morning, right? How do you think you did?" he asks her.

She responds,
"I feel like I did well."

They arrive at the restaurant where they eat and talk for nearly two hours before finally catching one of the evening's later shows. Reena's phone vibrates repeatedly until eventually, she turns it off, but before doing so she glances at the screw to see a text from Lock that reads "Can I talk to you please?" On the ride home they listen to a playlist that unbeknownst to Reena, Castle created specifically for her. Once back at her residence he walks Reena to the door-he surely wouldn't duplicate his gaffe from earlier. She turns her key to unlock the door and swings around with open arms as if to ask for a hug. Castle leans in and hugs her low as she grasps him around his neck. The embrace lasts longer than normal and they pull away from each other very slowly. Castle never relinquishes his hold as his arms slide back and his hands grip her waist. He pulls her close and gently kisses her where her neck meets her jawline. He then pecks the left side of her neck slowly before pulling his head back and pressing his lips against hers. For a split second, Reena hesitates but quickly reciprocates. Castle rubs his hands up and down her sides and around to the small of her back. The street is quiet, the slight sound of his idling engine produces the only background noise, yet a marching band is playing inside his head. He almost can't believe that she is kissing him back. Her body is so delicate yet firm. He pulls her to him until they a credit card could not swipe between them, yet he feels that she is not close enough. He then lowers his head and rests it in her shoulder as they softly rock back and forth still intertwined. She kisses him on the neck and says to him
"I gotta go in, I have to wake up early tomorrow."

She turns to go inside but before she could completely get around he grabs her by the hand and asks
"Can I come in?"

Chapter 16

YOU, ME, HIM AND HER

Every August, the annual city day in Salem takes place called "Market Street Day." Not unlike summer fests that take place all across the country, there are vendors, live music, games and an all around good time. One year, in an ode to Salem's history and the heroics of Robert Gibbon Johnson, a tomato throwing contest was held. Teams of two people hurled and caught the red fruit, with the toss managing to travel the furthest distance in the air while ultimately being caught undamaged was declared the winner. The contest began around 9 AM and would last all day. When Lock and Castle ran into Reena and Milan, they decided to try their luck at the game of pitch and catch. Normally there were two scenarios that took place. The teams were either divided into the boys against the girls, or Reena and Lock versus Castle and Milan. This day was the first to see that dynamic broken. Lock originally proposed that he and Castle team up as he didn't think that either girl would be able to throw far enough or catch a tomato coming in hot from twenty-five yards away. After the girls threw a fit, Lock acquiesced and chose Milan as his partner. Always looking to win, he felt that Milan was the better athlete and therefore gave him the best chance at victory.

Milan's strategy was to have Lock throw to her. It was much more likely that she would catch a long traveling tomato than to throw one. By 11:30 AM when the group stepped up to take their respective turns the best throw so far was a modest thirty-five feet. Lock understood however that it was early in the day and that many more people would pass through the celebration offering up their best heaves in hopes of earning the crown. Each team was given three throws, so Lock made his first attempt from sixty-five feet away. He stood there in a center fielders stance and hoisted the tomato high. He let it roll off of his fingertips as he tried to throw it as far as possible while still landing softly. Milan completely whiffed at it, never laying a hand on the tomato as is exploded just to the left of the double yellow line in the center of the closed-off street. After a mental retool, Lock determined that an underhanded delivery may have been better, so after a hop step he launched the tomato into the sky. This time Milan made a great effort to catch it, even lowering her cupped hands quickly as the tomato zoomed down into her waiting grasp. She failed to hold on as it slid out of her palms, over her wrists and in between her forearms before slapping to the ground.

"Concentrate." Lock yelled to her as he set up for his third and final attempt.

Milan gave him the "OK" signal with her fingers and stood in a semi-crouched position completely focused on catching the next tomato to come plummeting into her atmosphere. Again, after a quick hop Lock sends the red piece of food arching in Milan's direction. She never takes her eyes off of it as it descends into her hands. She caught it! After realizing that the tomato had not slipped from her clutch, Milan jumped up and down like she was storming the field after a World Series victory. The triumph was short-lived. After handing the tomato over to the judge, it was deemed damaged therefore disqualifying the effort. Next up, Castle and Reena.

After studying Lock and Milan's mistakes, Castle coached Reena on exactly how to catch the tomato. Reena wasn't the athlete that Milan was, but it was all about technique in Castle's mind. Lock and Milan stood near Reena so that they could coach her on how to correctly haul in the projectile. Just as Lock before him, Castle cast the tomato toward the heavens in an underhand motion. As it sailed toward Reena, directions also flew into her ear from Lock as he stood about ten yards to her left.

"Square your feet." he said.

"Get under it and keep your hands tucked. Keep your hands together and let it land soft." he stated as the tomato made its landing.

Like a bullseye, the tomato landed squarely into the center of her chest. Like a red bomb had been detonated on impact, tomato juice and chunks shot out in every direction. Lock fell to the ground in laughter causing Milan to crack up as well. Castle faired better, running around in circles as if he had just witnessed one of the funniest moments of his life. Even the judge let out a chuckle as he tried to hand Reena a napkin to wipe her face. She was so upset that she stormed off without one word. The other three hurried to catch up to her, Lock and Castle still howled like hyenas as they told her that it as OK.

"Where are you going?" Milan asked Reena as she raced toward Broadway.

"Home! I gotta change my clothes." she replied.

"Yeah, it's over for that shirt. You might as well throw that jawn away." Castle adds before another round of laughter.

"Forget y'all. It's not funny. You're always laughing at everything." Reena yelled.

Milan followed up by saying,

"Yeah y'all, just go back over there. We'll be back after she changes. Y'all are only making it worse."

"Well I said it was a bad idea. Should've listened." Lock said to them.

"We'll catch y'all when y'all get back." Castle said to the girls.

The boys went back to Market Street as Milan walked Reena home while assuring her that everything was fine. She wanted badly to be able to laugh like the boys, but she didn't want to hurt Reena's feelings. Especially since she was so excited about her outfit which was ruined on its first wear. The four of them did not hang out for the rest of the day. When the girls returned, Lock and Castle were among a group of ten boys from their football team running around and playing games together. Reena and Milan met up with a few girls from the neighborhood and ate food while they watched the boys and listened to music. Even though she eats pizza, Reena never stopped hating tomatoes after that day.

***

Lock barely left the house in the three weeks since his party, only venturing out and breathing fresh air five or six times at the most. After his fight with Castle, they haven't spoken once, and Reena still won't take any of his calls or respond to his texts. He stopped by her house once but she wasn't there, and a mixture of pride and frustration won't allow him to continually show up at her door unwelcomed. Without a clear sense on how to maneuver through a street beef, Lock has pretty much decided to hide until he can figure out his next move. Even in reclusion, the show must go on. Lock has a few meetings lined up today, still with the culmination of the events of his life burning down around him, he puts on a veneer of confidence and pretends to be comfortable inside the inferno.

Just before Lock loops the second turn of the double Windsor knot he is creating with his necktie, there is a knock at the door. He bumbles to the front of the house initially very nimbly, becoming more and more apprehensive with each step. Fearing a home invasion he creeps toward the entrance like a balanced feline. After a quick peak, the stress dissipates. He turns the knob and swings open the barrier-standing there on the front step is Milan holding a huge metal pot in her hand.

"Hey, what's going on?" Lock asks as he turns around to walk away knowing that she will enter behind.

"Oh, I forgot that you had business to take care of today. Well I ain't here for you anyway. I brought this for your GrandPop." Milan states.

"Oh word? That's how it's going down now?" Lock asks jokingly.

Milan responds,
"I'm just playing. It's enough in here for both of y'all."

"Yup! That's what I'm talking about." Lock states.
He rubs his hands together and asks
"So what is it?"

"Chicken Alfredo." Milan replies.
She puts the pot on the counter and tells Lock,
"I got some cheesy bread too, but I couldn't carry it all-it's sitting on my front seat."

Heading back to finish preparing Lock asks her,
"You want me to grab it or are you gonna get it? I'm trying to get ready, I gotta leave in a few minutes."

"It's OK, I'll get it." she says.

After grabbing his shoes, Lock comes back into the room and sits to put them on. He says to Milan,
"Thanks. I appreciate it. I appreciate you coming by and checking on me and my GrandPop. I got a lot of friends, but not many that I can trust, and with the whole thing with Reena plus me not talking to Castle either, I'm just kinda out here right now. I don't wanna talk your head off, but I just wanted to say that. I didn't expect you to be this cool."

"I understand. Well, things will get better no matter what. Just go out and kill your meetings, and I'll probably be here when you get back. If I gotta leave I'll come back by later, but I'm gonna go in here and talk to your GrandPop for a minute and like I said, I'll see you later." Milan replies.

"OK, cool." Lock says as he reaches for his jacket.

"And did he ever tell you about a show called, um, I Dream Of Jeannie or something like that?"

Lock laughs and asks
"Yeah, why?"

"Oh because I watched it with him yesterday when you was in there knocked out." Milan replies.

"Yeah, I used to watch a lot of those old shows. When I was a kid, like real little, like before I could tell time, I would sit on the bed and watch those shows before he went to work. He would tell me 'Wake me up when the big hand gets on the nine' and I would sit there and watch whatever was on his TV until it was time for me to get him up. I always turned the channel when McHale's Navy came on though. I never got into that one. It was cartoon time by then." Lock adds.

"So you knew that The Addams Family was a show before the movies?" Milan asks.

Locks laughs even louder.
"Yes, I knew that. I gotta go though, I'll mess around and be late fooling with you."

"OK, well text me when you're on your way and I'll put a plate in the microwave for you." Milan says just before Lock walks out.

"Alright, I will." he says

The most pressing matter Lock wants to tie up, other than the looming coup of his company, is getting Stylez under contract. This will give him the clear direction that he was looking for just before his ship sailed into troubled waters. He decides that he is going to approach his meeting with Stylez without any fluff. Straightforward and honest is the best way to go. He is meeting Stylez in Delaware at the Starbucks inside of the Christiana Mall. For Lock, this is a chance to let his guard down a little. If the sit down had been set in Salem he would be looking over his shoulder instead of totally focusing on the business. Here he has nothing to worry about and it is slightly refreshing. After parking, he is sure to pick up the manila folder sitting on the seat next to him. It contains the contract that he will be pushing for Stylez to sign so that they can officially get to work. The Starbucks is inside of Barnes & Noble so Lock browses a few books as he is an hour early.

"Can I help you find something?" a bookstore attendant asks Lock.

He looks up from his skimming and says to her
"No I'm fine. Just looking."

Then his face lights up and he says,
"As a matter of fact, do you have a book called The Spook Who Sat By The Door?"

"Uh, I don't know off hand, but if you walk over to the desk with me, I can look it up." she replies.

Once they reach the service desk she asks him,
"And who is the author?"

"Um, what is his name? Uh, Sam Greenlee I believe." he says.

After typing into the computer she informs Lock,
"We do have that, if you will follow me right over here I'll show you where it is.
"
"Thanks a lot." Lock states as he tails her to the location.

After purchasing the book, Lock sits at a table not far from the magazine section. He waits quietly while facing the door, deep into his mobster fantasy. When Stylez finally walks in, Lock rises to greet him. The two are seated and Lock wastes no time getting to the topic at hand.

"I'm just gonna be straight up with you, Stylez. I'm not gonna act like you need us more than we need you. I'm here to tell you we need you, but nobody will go hard for you like me. I told you all about the things that we have lined up the last time we talked, and you see how lit the party was not too long ago. I'm here to tell you that with us on the same page, we can blow the roof off and change the game. Now I have a copy of the contract that I gave you right here and I'm hoping that you will sign it right now. I have another meeting after this and it will be ten times better if this is already secured before I get there. I don't wanna rush you, but it would be great if we could get this outta the way and get to work."

Lock spins the folder around so that the contents now face Stylez. He places a black free-flowing pen onto the table next to the folder. Stylez flips through the papers rather quickly and signs without hesitation.

"You won't regret this. I'm gonna make us both rich." he tells Stylez.

"That's what I like to hear!" Stylez replies.

"It's not all about money though. What we're really chasing is the creation of something great. If we create something that's special, the money will come, but on top of that we'll live forever and that's the goal." Lock says.

"Well let's do it!" Stylez says to him.

After parting with Stylez, Lock must now travel back to Salem where he is scheduled to update Scott Campbell on the present state of the label. He arrives in good spirits and assured Scott that everything is moving according to plan, even boasting of the newest artist signed to the company. After a breakdown of potential numbers and the promise of another meeting in the very near future, Lock was on his way. This is the best that Lock has felt in nearly a month, but as peaceful as he feels, he knows that it will not last. There is a huge cloud following him around and he is aware that precipitation is sure to follow. He arrives late to find the speech that he was looking to catch nearly over.

"Like I said before, I wasn't always who you see standing here today. I was not a good man by any stretch of the imagination. I was everything that is tearing this community apart-in my actions, and more importantly in my thinking. I've left that lifestyle behind me, but now! Now I walk amongst the evil for the greater good. Now I may ask you to walk with me at times because to take on issues like poverty, income inequality, the lack of educational resources and all of the other things eat away at the soul of these neighborhoods, well, no one can win alone. I do promise each of you that I will always be front and center for this battle as we take these streets back. Thank you very much."

Applause and adulation can be heard from the small audience
as the man ends his speech. He is greeted as he steps down and carries on a few quick conversations before finally seeing Lock and walking over to
him.
"Lock! How is everything young

brother?" Deuce asks.

"Why do you call me young brother when you're not too much older than me?" Lock asks.
"I've lived life at such a fast pace that I feel about eighty years old." Deuce replies.

The two men share a quick laugh before Deuce looks at Lock and says,
"I call you young because I am jealous of the innocence that I see all over your face.   You're grown, but I love how the streets never corrupted you."

"I guess I can thank you for helpling me stay focused." Lock replies.

"I tried to help when I could, but at the end of the day you made the right choices." he says.

Lock giggles and says to him,
"All I see are the mistakes. You did help me a lot though. I hope you know."

"Just like your Dad did for me. I don't know what he saw in me, but he put me under his wing and nobody could touch me. I was a youngin' out there blowing in the wind. He always pushed me away from the street life, but I ran to it every chance I got. I feel like he saved my life, so the least I could do was look out for his son once he passed." Deuce said as he put his hand on Lock's shoulder.

Lock looks at the floor and responds,
"People tell me stories, but I don't really remember him."

"He'd definitely be proud of the way you turned out. He didn't want you in these streets." Deuce tells him.

After a brief silence, he asks
"I didn't know you were coming by, though. What brings you here today? Did you come by to get inspired for the struggle or what?"

"I just wanted to kick it about a few things. I got a lot up in the air right now, and I feel like I'm at a crossroads. The next few decisions I make could either make me or break me. Since I really respect your opinion, I wanted to see what you thought." Lock pleads.

"Oh, okay. Council to the boss. Consigliere! Well what is troubling you young Godfather?" he asks.

Lock leans in close and whispers in his ear
"I need a gun."

Across town, Castle and Reena have fallen into a routine of movies, eating out, TV shows and cooking. Sprinkled in between are the times that Castle helps Reena study for her classes, and he taught her how to shoot craps and play blackjack in preparation for a trip to Atlantic City. As they sit on the couch watching TV and playing Words With Friends, Reena asks Castle,
"You know what? Did you order that gift for your Mom? You told me to remind you."

"Yeah, I ordered her a new suitcase. It's like one of those bulletproof suitcases. Ballistic I think they call it. I ordered it, they said it'll be here either tomorrow or the next day. I didn't check the tracking yet though." Castle replies.

"Bulletproof. Why would she need that? You're always into some gangster stuff." Reena says.

"It's not that. You know since she got that new job she's always traveling. Literally, like all of the time. So that time they had the shooting in the airport, my Mom was in that airport that day. Luckily her flight just left right before the guy started shooting. So I was looking at the news and calling her phone back to back to back. It kept going straight to voicemail and the more it did the more I panicked. I called her about fifty times and sent about fifty texts. They were in the air so her phone didn't have service. When she finally landed then her phone was blowing up with message after message from me and then she starts to panic. She called me thinking somebody was dead. So I thought that would be a good idea just in case. You never know. She may have to use it as a shield one day. Just like we say out in the streets it's better to have it and not need it than to need it and not have it. It should be here in time for her birthday, I gotta sign for it at the house though." Castle states.

"Well, that makes sense when you put it like that. You know what else? Do you even have a home anymore? You're always here. When I left earlier I started to look in your car to see if all of your clothes were in there, but it wasn't out front. Thought maybe you got evicted or something." Reena jokes.

"Hardy har har." Castle mocks.

"Seriously though, you haven't even went to hang out or do any of that street stuff. I'm not complaining about that, I think you need to leave it alone anyway, but it's just weird. You better not be in trouble. Are you hiding out or something?" Reena asks.
  Quick to cover up his nervousness at Reena's question, he responds,
  "Nah, everything is cool. I'm just staying away from the streets right now, plus I like being around you."

"Awe, that's so sweet." she says.
  She leans in and kisses him on the cheek. He slides his hand in between her back and the cushion. He inches closer and pulls her in the rest of the way. He kisses in succession from the base of her neck up to the side of her face until eventually, they lock lips. He slowly flips the bottom of her shirt with his fingertips and begins to lift it upward. Just as her shirt circles her rib cage, she snatches it down as she pulls away from Castle. She says to him,
  "I told you, not yet."

Lock lands home after a long day to find Milan asleep in his bed. Inside of the serenity, he sees a beauty in her that he never saw before. Her abrasive personality coupled with the glare from Reena's light in Lock's life never allowed him to view her as he does in this moment. She has been so good to him lately that he almost wants to kiss her as she sleeps. He goes into the kitchen and as promised a plate of food is in the microwave. He heats up the food and grabs a bottle of water from the refrigerator. He loosens his tie and unbuttons the top button of his shirt while he waits for the ding of the microwave timer. After the countdown is complete, he heads back to the bedroom where he slowly places the plate on the nightstand and sits gently on the bed while making a concerted effort to not wake Milan from her peaceful slumber. He slides off his dress shoes and an instant relaxation rushes over him. He pulls a t-shirt and a pair of basketball shorts from his dresser and quickly changes clothes. Normally he would hang his suit, but after such an eventful day he lays it on the dresser assigning that task to another day. He sits on the bed with his back against the headboard, one leg stretched out and the other on the floor. He attacks the plate of food like a Great White tearing away at a wounded sea otter. The clanging of the fork against the plate as he returns it to the nightstand wakes Milan. In a groggy voice, she asks,
  "When did you get here? Why didn't you wake me up?"

"You looked like that sleep was so good that I didn't wanna bother you." Lock replies.

"Did everything go good?" she asks.

"Yeah, for the most part." Lock says to her.

She rolls over and sits up, then asks,
"You wanna talk about it?"

Lock's phone vibrates on the bed between them. He picks it up but does not recognize the number, so he immediately sends it to voicemail. As he lays the phone back down onto the bed it begins to vibrate again with the call coming from the same number. He again clicks the button on the side of his phone, prematurely prompting the mystery caller to leave him a message. After dropping the device onto his maroon comforter a text message comes through, followed by another and quickly another. They read:
"Sorry it's so late, I had to ask around to get your number."

"I'm trying to help you."

"We need to talk ASAP. This is Schemer."

Chapter 17

I GAVE YOU POWER

1986 was a polarizing year. Run-DMC cemented Hip Hop as a viable genre, releasing their triple platinum album Raising Hell. Mike Tyson punched his way into immortality becoming the youngest heavyweight boxing champion in history, and a couple of disasters claimed the headlines with the nuclear meltdown at Chernobyl, and the Space Shuttle Challenger which blew up on live television just seconds after takeoff. A positive explosion hit Salem in the form of celebration as the boys' high school basketball team brought home the city's first state championship in nearly twenty years. Attica was too young to attend the game, but the stories were legendary. He knew that Salem took on Newark's Central High on the floor of the basketball arena at Rutgers University. He also knew that the Rams put up an all-time great performance against Asbury Park to earn a spot in the championship game, and would cut down the nets after a 77-63 thumping of the Blue Devils. A few years later Attica was blessed with the opportunity to watch a tape of the game during an inclement weather procedure at school. Salem has a storied history of exceptional athletes and teams packed to the brim with talent. What made the 1986 team so loved and remembered was the cast of characters. So individually adored that the entire roster could be called out by nickname anywhere in the city and no explanation was needed for whom the moniker belonged to. Names like Six-Nine, City, Womp and Sita. The most lovable player on the team was a giant, well over three hundred pounds named Pat Pat who could toss a man clear across the room with the wave of an arm, but much rather preferred to laugh and have fun. The motor that made the championship vehicle fly was a tall, lanky prototype-a point forward before Scottie Pippen or LeBron James. They called this athletic freak "Star." He could push the ball coast to coast controlling the leather sphere as if it were attached to a string, finishing with a juke step and a glide to the basket before hammering down a violent dunk. He would not only lead the team to the title, but he would end his career as the schools all-time leading scorer. To Attica and his friends, these guys were superstars. Like every kid growing up in those days, they all idolized Michael Jordan, Magic Johnson and Doctor J. Even more than those NBA superstars, the boys in his neighborhood picked up a ball because they wanted to be Star, City and Pat Pat.

A milk carton with the bottom cut out, nailed to a tree with a square piece of plywood in between may as well have been the Boston Garden to Attica and his friends. They played for hours on end dribbling a miniature basketball in the dirt yard with as much passion as Larry Bird bouncing the roundball to the famed parquet floor. Most games started with a debate over who would be each player from the '86 championship team. After making some sense of the dire issue, the game could finally begin. Attica hates to lose and on this day, his team was getting crushed. To make matters worse, there were an even number of players present which meant that no one was waiting on the sidelines to play, so the teams remained the same. After three losses Attica was close to blowing a gasket. He proposed that the teams be switched but no one from the winning squad wanted to change sides. More determined than ever, he decided to play his heart out and bring home a win even if he had to make every basket and rebound every miss. In the end, his efforts were not enough and though much more competitive, his team came up short. Attica was so irate that he threw Jamar's ball over a fence two houses away. Under normal circumstances, that's not a problem, many basketballs as well as footballs and baseballs landed in neighbors' yards at times. Making this situation dramatically different were the two large doberman pinschers that lived there. Not only were they big, but they were as mean as a mama wasp. With no way to get past the boy-eating gatekeepers, the game was over and Attica did not care. His emotions always had a tendency to take over and he would ruin everything without batting an eye.

***

After rapping on the door to New's apartment for much longer than he would like, Schemer is finally granted access when Attica answers to let him in.
"Damn man, what took you so long?" Schemer asks.

"Chill, I was in the bathroom." Attica replies.

Schemer sits on the couch and leans back comfortably. He locks his fingers as his hands rest on the crown of his head and he asks,
"You heard from News?"

"Yeah, he called earlier. Nothing new. I talked to his lawyer yesterday, he said he's gonna file a motion to try to get him a bail, but right now he just gotta sit. That bail reform law stung him, so now if his lawyer can't pull a trick outta his hat this dude might not hit the streets until it's settled." Attica says.

"Well what's the plan for the stuff that he was working on?" Schemer asks.

"I don't really wanna talk about that right now." Attica snaps.

"I'm just saying. I don't know if you plan to use Little E but I don't think you should." Schemer pleads.

Attica perks up a bit and says to Schemer
"I don't trust them little dudes. They roll with News, that's fine, but all his friends ain't my friends, just like all of your friends ain't my friends. Remember that. Them

little niggas is quick to put in work, but they ain't battle tested. They might fold under pressure and tell everything. Keep them away from me-I don't want them to know about nothing that I'm doing."

"Yeah, I feel you on that. I was thinking though. If Castle goes, what's to stop the other one from just packing up and leaving? Like I said before, he's a college kid, he don't really know what's going on. Castle is the only way in if that's still what you want. I know that you said you don't wanna talk about it, but I gotta tell you what I think is best. You think that college kid is really gonna sit at the table and just let you in? He'd probably run and never come back. Keep Castle alive so that he lets you in and then once you have the hooks in, you can kill him or let him live, it won't matter either way. Right now though, it's too soon. Everything is over if he's gone." Schemer says.

"I ain't really trying to hear that right now. If it gets handled it gets handled, if it don't, it don't. But all that dealmaking shit ain't always the way, and it ain't always about getting every dollar. My name is worth more than money out here." Attica says aggressively.

"Woah Kemosabe, no need to get all upset, but it wouldn't be right if I didn't say what I think is right." Schemer says.

"Kemosabe? You listen to that corny ass song?" Attica asks.

"Nah, it's from The Lone Ranger. I saw the movie not too long ago. I heard it was a remake though, I never saw the old one. I think it was out when my GrandMom was little or something so you know I ain't watching that shit." Schemer laughs.

After typing into his phone, Schemer rises to his feet and says to Attica,
"I gotta roll though. I got a bunch of stuff to do. Just hit me if you need me, if not I'll be back through a little bit later. Are you gonna be here?"

"Depends on what time. I'm taking Tiff to pick up some clothes for RJ. She asked for the bread, but I ain't about to give her money and let her do whatever. We can pick out these clothes together, plus I can make sure that she don't pick out a bunch of bullshit. If I ain't here, just get with me tomorrow. I'll hit you up though." Attica replies.

Schemer is surprised by Attica's response but makes sure that no outward signs show. Attica never dismisses anything until the next day. He always has a phone near and will answer no matter what. With not much time to prod around and figure out what is going on, Schemer asks,

"Yo, is there a umbrella here? It might rain in a little bit and I'm gonna a be out and about."

"What the hell would I be doing with umbrellas laying around. Suck it up and get wet. I can tell you ain't no true hustler. I used to be outside in any weather. Rain don't stop nothing" Attica replies.

"OK, so no? Cool. I'll check you out later." Schemer adds as he exits.

Castle never knew that a grilled cheese made on a Foreman Grill could taste so wonderful. Reena's secret was to butter both sides of the bread. She then lays down a single slice, placing the cheese on top. After thirty seconds or so she adds the second slice of bread and closes the lid to the grill. A crispy golden masterpiece will emerge not long after, and Castle's first experience was magic to his taste buds. After devouring a new spin on an old classic, Castle cleaned the dishes before turning the house upside down for twenty minutes looking for Reena's car keys.

"How do you lose these things every day?" he asks.

"Leave me alone boy." she replies.

"No seriously, it's like you hide them from yourself or something. Either that or a ghost moves them." he says to her.

She smacks him on the arm and says "Don't say that. I'll never be able to sleep in here again."

"Can you take me to pick up my car real quick? It's supposed to rain later and if I gotta run out I don't want to have to walk to get my car, and you act all funny about getting wet so I don't wanna have to ask you to come out." Castle pleads.

"Yeah, come on." Reena replies.

"Can you follow me right back here though and let me in? I'm just gonna chill here 'til later." he asks.

"Yeah, that's fine, but come on, I gotta go." she states.

When the two reach Castle's house he notices a sticky note on the front door. He dashes up to retrieve it and reads that it is a notice of missed delivery. He heads back down the walkway and over to the passenger window of Reena's idling vehicle.

"This is from the post office. I gotta run up there and pick up my Mom's gift. They tried to deliver it but it needed a signature so I gotta go up there and get it. Just give me your key and I'll be there when you get back." Castle says.

"You better not lose my key." Reena responds as she twists her house key from the metal ring connecting it to her car fob.

"I won't. I'll see you when you get back." he replies.

"I have a few things to do so I won't be back for a few hours. Call me or text me if you have to leave and if I'm close enough I'll come get my key." Reena states.

As Castle backs away from the car, he says to her,
"Alright, see you later."

~

The vibration of Lock's phone creates an intermittent drum pattern against the stained wood of his nightstand. He rushes into the bedroom to take the call but is seconds too late.

"Why didn't you tell me that my phone was ringing?" Lock asks Milan.

"I was gonna tell you when you came back in here." she replies.

"I thought I heard it, but I wasn't sure. It took a second for me to realize it." he says.

He presses the number to return the call before placing the phone to his ear.
"Yo, what's up?" he asks.

On the other end of the phone is Schemer, who asks Lock,
"What's up man, we still good to meet up today?"

"Yeah that's cool." Lock responds.
"Alright, you wanna come to me or do you want me to come to you?" Schemer asks.

"I'm in Delaware right now. You can just meet me over here. That would be best for me." Lock states.

Schemer says to him
"OK, it's a go. Where at?"

"Meet me at The Christiana Mall in the food court. I'll be right by Suki Hana. Be there around 5:30." Lock says.

He hangs up the phone and Milan immediately asks,
"Why did you lie and say you're in Delaware?"

"So much is going on you probably wouldn't believe me if I told you." Lock says to her.
He sits on the bed resting his hands in his lap. He then raises his hands to his face with one palm covering each eye and crashes back onto the bed like a mighty redwood bowing to the lumberjack's ax.

"Listen, and I mean really listen. It's important. If I don't come back, let everybody know that I'm going to meet Schemer. I told him I was already in Delaware because I don't know what's going on. I don't think it's a setup, but I'm not sure." he says.

Milan stands to her feet, shocked by the seriousness of Lock's statement, she asks
"What do you mean if you don't come back?"

"I don't think it's that anything is gonna happen, at least not yet, but I'm letting you know just in case." he says.

"Well what's going on? You're not leaving out that door without telling me more than that. I swear to God I'll follow you to Delaware." she claims.

"It's a long story, but I'm kinda stressed out, I'm not even thinking straight. I even thought about getting a gun." Lock says to her.

"Now you know you don't even play like that." she replies.

"I know, and it's not like I'm trying to just run up and shoot somebody, but I feel like I'm out here like a sitting duck right now. What can I do when I got people after me who don't play by any rules? That's why I thought about it, but I went over to see Deuce and he talked me out of it." he says.

"Who?" Milan asks.

"Deuce. You probably don't know him by that name. His real name is Mike Winston, he is like an activist now, but he was a young boy that my Dad used to take care of in the streets so he always looks out for me." Lock tells her.

"Oh yeah, I know who you're talking about. He was on the front page of the paper when all of them people got killed in the same week." Milan states.

"Yeah, that's him. They used to call him Deuce back in the day, so that's what I know him as. When I was a kid, he used to give me money and buy me stuff. Now I go by to talk to him sometimes, and when I asked him for that gun I almost had to fight him. He let me have it. I didn't get into the whole story with him behind why I asked, but I might have to go back and tell him." Lock says.

"Well what about Castle, he can't help you? He carries guns sometimes, right?" she asks.

Lock dismissively waves his hand.

"Man, he's the reason why this whole thing is going down now. What happened was, apparently when we started the label, way back before I left to go to college, he borrows some money from the guy Attica, the one that was at the club a few weeks ago.."

Milan cuts in and says

"Oh yeah, they sat at the table with us almost all night. You better watch out for them. I didn't really know them before that night, but I heard later that he just came home from jail and that one of them likes to shoot people."

"Yeah, I know. So like I was saying, he borrowed the money from him that he used to help me start the company, now this guy wants part of the company! I don't even know him. I saw him around, but I don't know him. So now I think they sent somebody to kill Castle a few weeks ago, but I'm not sure. I really don't know what's going on so I'm meeting with the boy Schemer to see if I can calm it down somehow. So when I leave, remember everything I told you. I wanted to meet at the mall because it's always packed and I don't think they would try anything right there." Lock says to her.

"Oh my God, I'm so scared. My hands are shaking." Milan says.

After a deep breath, Lock says to her,
"Well, I don't really know what to expect, but my gut is telling me that it's not a setup. I could be wrong, but I'm usually right with the vibes that I get."

The entire ride to Delaware is silent. The light drizzle tapping the roof and windshield act as white noise, lulling Lock further into a zone as he journeys to concert with an advocate of his situational hell. Feeling more like Henry Hill on his way to meet Jimmy at the diner, Lock arrives early and sits facing the entrance. His eyes are glued to the people flowing in and out, so much so that he does not glance at his phone once.

A few minutes before 5 o'clock in glides Schemer. He is alone, but Lock keeps his eyes to the entrance in case others file in behind him. Lock stands to his feet and raises his hand in order to be located, then retakes his seat and once again focuses on the door.
"What's up?" Schemer asks.

"I don't know. You tell me." Lock replies.

"Well you seem like a smart dude, so I ain't even gonna beat around the bush. You got a problem, and I can help you with that problem." Schemer states.

"So how are you gonna do that, and why?" Lock asks.

He sits up a little straighter and reiterates,
"Why just help me? Out of the kindness of your heart? Or are you just coming with more of Attica's threats?"

"I look at it like this, you have two choices because Attica is pretty intent on blowing some shit up. The first choice is, you can work with me. Hear me out. Attica wanted an equal share in your company just because. You will be paying him and he won't bring any value. Between three people that means you'd be giving him a third of the company. Give me ten percent and not only will I make the whole situation go away, but I'll also bring assets to your brand. I'm assuming that your business is totally legit and has paperwork?"

Lock nods yes.

"Well, in that case, I can maybe even secure an office building, and I won't deal in your everyday activities. Option number two is to try this on your own and see how long you last. It's by the grace of God that Castle ain't dead already, but to tell you the truth, it's only a matter of time. If News didn't get bagged he'd probably be toe-tagged already. Once Castle is buried who do you think they're gonna come for? You think Attica is gonna go for anything but you bowing down? You think News is gonna listen to your reasoning when he got a gun in your face? You can either rock with me and have a peaceful situation that's much better anyway, or you can get on some gangsta shit and go to war. Your choice." Schemer tells him.

Lock sits with his elbows pressed hard to the table, fingers locked into a ball just under his nose.

"I need some time to think about it." he says.

"There is a tide in the affairs of men." Schemer replies.

"What do you mean by that?" Lock asks.

"I thought you would know that, college kid. It's from Julius Caesar. The saying is longer, but it basically means that just like a ship's only chance to come and go is with the tide, so are the chances in the business that men do. You gotta take the opportunity when it comes, if not, it might be over for you. Read it one day." Schemer states.

He gets up from the table and slides his chair in. He says to Lock,
"I'll give you 'til tomorrow to make a decision. Don't wait too long."

In less than a minute he is gone from view. After sitting in a daze for a few minutes, Lock gets up and walks directly over to Barnes & Noble.